"STOP BEING SO POSSESSIVE OF ME!" IRISH CRIED.

"I'm not being possessive. All I asked was why didn't you leave me a note telling me where you were," Geoff retorted.

"Why don't you get a dog? Put him on a leash. I'm not your pet. I'm not at your beck and call." She saw her words hitting deep, hurting him. "You said you wanted an independent woman. Clearly you don't. You want an ornament for your life. Go find a clinging vine."

"That's not fair, Irish, and you know it. Is it so wrong to wonder where you are and worry about you?"

"Yes! You know what the problem is as well as I do. You treat me as if I can't get through life without you. I'm going to get run over by a car, fall into a manhole, wander around lost like a child. I don't know what goes on in that crazy head of yours, but I know this: I can't live with it!"

CANDLELIGHT ECSTASY ROMANCES®

A
WHISPER
AWAY

Beverly Wilcox Hull

A CANDLELIGHT ECSTASY ROMANCE®

Published by
Dell Publishing Co., Inc.
1 Dag Hammarskjold Plaza
New York, New York 10017

ISBN: 0-440-19576-4

Printed in the United States of America

First printing—November 1985

To Our Readers:

We have been delighted with your enthusiastic response to Candlelight Ecstasy Romances®, and we thank you for the interest you have shown in this exciting series.

In the upcoming months we will continue to present the distinctive, sensuous love stories you have come to expect only from Ecstasy. We look forward to bringing you many more books from your favorite authors and also the very finest work from new authors of contemporary romantic fiction.

As always, we are striving to present the unique, absorbing love stories that you enjoy most—books that are more than ordinary romance. Your suggestions and comments are always welcome. Please write to us at the address below.

Sincerely,

The Editors
Candlelight Romances
1 Dag Hammarskjold Plaza
New York, New York 10017

ONE

She was on horseback, regal, exuding power, her hand extended toward the white-robed figure. There was triumph in her eyes, but also gladness, pride, relief, and, yes, compassion.

Irish O'Brien studied her painting. She was seeking to capture the moment when Queen Isabella accepted the surrender of Granada in 1492, ending a thousand years of Moorish rule in Spain, but something was missing. Then she knew. Nodding decisively, she selected a brush and dipped the tip in paint, then deftly added a small tear glistening in the eye of the Moorish caliph. Yes, just the right touch. And it was true. The caliph had wept as he surrendered the keys to his beloved Granada.

Aloud she said, "Poor man. I almost feel sorry for him, but then Granada really wasn't his city. It belonged to Spain."

She felt a movement at her feet and looked down at Sam, who had sat up at the sound of her voice. A handsome golden Labrador, Sam wasn't just a dog. He was her best friend and occasional art critic.

"You don't think the caliph ought to cry? Okay, his mother didn't either." She lifted the painting from the easel and held it down to the dog. "See, Sam? She's the lady in black behind the caliph. When she saw his tears she said, 'Weep, son. Weep like a woman for what you would not defend like a man.' Now there was a real tough lady, Sam. Good thing Isabella didn't have to fight *her.*"

Irish watched Sam raise his ears and cock his head to the side. "So what do you think, love? Is Isabella properly heroic?" The dog furrowed his brow as though worried. "I'm with you, darlin'. It had better be good. This job is an important part of our livelihood for the next year." That was certainly true. A major oil company had launched an ad campaign to honor women rulers throughout history. Irish had been commissioned as illustrator, and the pay was exceptional.

She bent and patted Sam, pulling gently at his floppy ears. He barked and ran toward the door. "You want to go out?" She shook her head in mock exasperation. "Nobody asks you to lie at my feet while I work. It's your own fault if you have cabin fever." She glanced at the clock on the mantel over the fireplace, an eight-day, chiming Little Ben which had been her mother's. A little before three. Heavens, she'd worked right through lunch. For a moment she was torn between the refrigerator and an impatient Sam. Then she stood up. "All right, my darling. I'm putty in your paws."

She stripped off her smock and hung it over the Isabella painting on her easel, then went to the bedroom and changed into her faded gray sweat suit. As she sat on the edge of the bed to put on her sweat socks and running shoes, Sam carried on in the doorway, barking, jumping up and down, barely able to restrain his eagerness.

"Patience, sweetie. You males are all alike. Can't wait to have your way with the poor working girl."

Irish often wondered how much Sam understood. She made a point of talking to him a lot. She needed the practice—and who else was there to talk to? But she refused to fall into the trap of believing Sam understood much more than the tone of her voice. "You aren't people. You're just a plain old mutt of dubious ancestry. Your mother was a pure-bred Lab, all right, a society girl, but she had the morals of an alley cat. Got out and was swept off her feet by a boxer, I suspect. So what's that make you? A boxer from Labrador?" She stood up and stamped her feet to perfect the fit of the Nikes. "C'mon, champ, you need your roadwork. I should've called you Champ. Sam is a dumb name."

Her house, cottage really, consisted of one large room which she used as a combination studio and sitting room, a tiny kitchen open to the main room except for a two-stool snack bar, and a smallish bedroom joined by a bath. The place was hope-lessly cluttered with books and the paraphernalia of her work. And it wasn't the warmest place in winter unless she kept the fireplace roaring. But the cottage had one distinct advantage. Her back door opened right onto Compo Beach at Westport, Connecticut.

This she now did and Sam bolted outside. He dashed directly for the beach. Irish followed as fast as she could. Sam ran like the wind and there was no leisurely jog with him. She had to sprint just to keep up with him. Oh well, it was good for the figure.

Twenty minutes later, after traversing the length of the beach three times, her sweat suit was nearly black with sweat and she was back in the house, winded but invigorated. While Sam lapped fresh water, she drank a glass of orange juice. "You're going to be the death of me, Sam. Why didn't I get a Chihuahua or a toy poodle?"

Sam's lapping stopped and he bolted into the

living room, heading for the front door this time. Thinking what a good doorbell he was, Irish followed.

"When are you going to listen to me and get a telephone, Irish? I hate dropping in like this."

Irish smiled at the face through the screen door. Doris Parkins was forever scolding her about something, yet she did it with such good humor and undeniable affection who could mind it? Doris was somewhere in her mid- to late thirties, a redhead, slim, imperious, and forever chic. Even in her diminutive white tennis dress she looked elegant.

Delighted to have unexpected company, Irish unlatched the screen and stood back. "I told you. A phone is a distraction. Who can work if it rings every five minutes?"

As always Doris had the last word. "Only someone with long-suffering friends who'll drive all the way over here to invite her for tennis." This sort of friendly banter was frequent between them and Irish loved it.

As Doris entered, Irish saw she was not alone. Following her into the room was perhaps the handsomest man she had ever seen. He was tall, at least six-two, with wavy, dark blond hair and dazzling blue eyes. But he was not "pretty handsome," as she thought of it. His face was too tanned and rugged for that, with a pronounced brow above deep-set eyes, and a prominent, squarish chin with a deep cleft in the middle. Above it was a delectable mouth. The upper lip was firm, almost straight, the lower lip fuller and more turned out. The effect of him was pure masculinity, aided no doubt by his tennis outfit which showed off his hard, well-toned body. She guessed he was in his mid-thirties.

Doris spoke, turning an open hand to encompass

this stranger. "Irish, this is—" She stopped in irritation. "Will you quiet that mutt? I can't get a word in edgewise."

Irish looked down at Sam. "If you'd just say hi to him. . . ." But she reached down and put her hand on his snout to quiet him. To Doris she said, "He can't help it if he likes you—for reasons impossible to understand."

"Dogs have good taste," Doris retorted before resuming the introduction. "Irish O'Brien, meet Geoffrey Winter. He's a college friend of Derek's up for the weekend and spells Jeff as G-E-O-F-F— for reasons which I'm sure are mysterious." She smiled. "I must say, if I'd known my husband had such a handsome friend, I never would have settled for the lesser of two evils."

Geoff Winter laughed at Doris, but his eyes were on Irish. She felt enveloped by them, somehow ensnared in intimacy. He held her gaze for what seemed a long time, then she was aware of his extended hand. When she took it she felt its cool, smooth, overpowering strength. What would it feel like, she immediately wondered, to have his strong hands roving over her entire body?

Unnerved by her own outrageous thought, she withdrew her hand and looked away from him, down at her sweat suit which was soaked and plastered against her body. She had a vision of her stringy hair. She looked back at him, saying nervously, "I must look—"

"Like you've been exercising." His smile was wide, displaying brilliant white teeth. "Taking your dog for a run on the beach, no doubt. What's his name?"

She had the sensation that Doris Parkins did not exist and Irish O'Brien and Geoff Winter were the

only persons in her cottage. It was with some diffi-
culty that she managed to say, "Sam. His name is
Sam."

"Good name. He looks like a Sam."

She watched as he squatted before Sam and gave
his head and ears a good rub. It wasn't fair. This
man was perfect. He was as handsome as the devil
and he also liked dogs. Sam, the traitorous beast,
loved the attention, wagging his tail in a wide arc.
He ought to growl or something. Geoff Winter
looked up at her. "I can see why you're called
Irish."

"Because my name is O'Brien?"

He relinquished Sam and stood up. She had such
a sense of his nearness. "I was thinking of your Irish
coloring—black hair like polished onyx, luminous
sapphire eyes, and a complexion Snow White might
have envied."

His words almost took her breath away. There
was a humorous twinkle in his eye, yet there could
be no doubt of his sincerity. This man found her
attractive—even in her present condition. The
thought was exciting—and dangerous. She sought
a rejoinder. "You must be a poet, Mr. Winter."

"Geoff, please—and I'm no poet, just a lawyer
with a discerning eye."

She could laugh now. "That's not how I came to
be called Irish. My Christian name is Iris. My little
sister couldn't pronounce it and I became—"

"Irish. It still fits you."

Again she felt ensnared by the intimacy of his
gaze. For relief she glanced at Doris who said impatiently, "I knew you two would get along, but you're
going to have to postpone your flirting until after
we play some tennis."

Irish glanced down at her sweat suit. "I'm sorry. If I'd known—but Sam just ran my legs off."

"Don't tell me you're too tired, Irish. We want you for a fourth even if you have to crawl around the court."

Irish glanced back at Geoff in time to see his lips forming the words, "—don't you agree?"

"I'm sorry. I was distracted. What did you say?"

He smiled. "I said that if we lose we'll certainly have a good excuse."

Doris pushed her toward the bedroom. "Hurry and change. We'll wait."

Irish hesitated. She really wanted to go, but she needed privacy to shower and change, and didn't want to have them waiting and rushing her. She smiled. "Tell you what. You go back and warm up. I'll meet you—" she glanced at the clock "—at four, not one minute later."

Doris Parkins sighed. "All right, but you'd better not be late. And wear your swimsuit under your whites. We'll take a dip afterward." She turned and handed her car keys to Geoff. "Be a love and drive, will you?"

When he was out the door she turned to Irish and whispered. "Isn't he a hunk? And he's loaded, too. You'd better not let this one get away, dearie."

In the kitchen Irish finished the last of her orange juice, watching Sam return to his water bowl. "What'd you think of him, Sam? I know. You fell in love. He called you beautiful, petted you, and you stood there wagging your whole body. Fine example you set." The dog quieted his lapping and looked quickly at her, as though deciding whether she was saying anything important. His return to the bowl signified he didn't think so.

"Can't blame you, I guess. He certainly is handsome and he does have a way with words. Hair like polished onyx, sapphire eyes—indeed! He had me quivering like a schoolgirl."

She poured herself a little more juice and sipped it thoughtfully. "Well, I'm not. I'm twenty-eight years old, a successful illustrator. Besides, we've been to this well once before, haven't we, Sam?"

Visions of Hank Peters flitted through her mind, so handsome, his body glistening from the surf, sinewy arms she could not deny. Ever since her parents and sister were killed in a plane crash, loneliness had been a chronic problem for her—until Hank Peters. He had been a balm for her isolation, someone to touch, hold, be held by. But it didn't last, it couldn't. Now in her inner vision she saw a horrid face, twisted in rage, screaming terrible words at her. When he left, her loneliness had been almost unbearable, but with her work, Sam, and the help of friends like Doris Parkins she had created a happy life.

"Yes, we're doing just fine, Sam. We're content. But there's no reason we can't circulate a bit. A tennis game with a handsome, *very* appealing stranger can't harm anything, can it? Bark once if you agree." The dog continued to lap his water.

It was a superb tennis match. Derek and Doris Parkins were among the best mixed doubles pairs in Westport and on their own private clay court they were nearly unbeatable. Irish knew she wouldn't have a chance, especially since she was so tentative and nervous at the start, except that Geoff Winter played like a pro. He hit hard and had a wicked serve. She was surprised at how much natural grace he had for a big man and how well he covered the court.

But no amount of effort by him could compensate for her bad play at the outset. She felt out of sync and missed shots which ordinarily would have been easy for her. She knew what the trouble was—him! The moment she arrived she saw the admiration in his eyes, and it made her self-conscious. She had such a sense that he was watching her every move—and there were lots of those. Never before had she realized just how much she jiggled while playing tennis. Why, oh why, had she worn this form-fitting blue shell and tiny tennis skirt.

But he was patient with her, encouraging her, telling her she'd get the next point. He wanted to win—he and Derek had been teammates on the Williams College tennis team and were very competitive with each other—but he wouldn't be a spoilsport if they didn't. Finally, she was able to concentrate and her game improved. Derek and Doris won both sets—what else was new?—but she and Geoff gave them all they could handle.

He was ecstatic in his praise. "You're fantastic. I can imagine how good you would have been if you hadn't run earlier. We almost won."

She enjoyed his praise, but his hand on her shoulder made her uneasy. There was nothing wrong with the gesture, she knew. It was just a simple display of camaraderie between team players, but it stirred up an uncomfortable yearning deep inside her, making her acutely aware of her femininity and his very pronounced masculinity.

"You must be beat."

She smiled up at him. "I am, but I think I've just enough energy for a *leisurely* dip in the pool."

"C'mon. You need a life raft."

On the short walk to the pool they spoke of their good plays and how close they'd come to victory.

15

"That water looks good," he yelled and ran ahead, stripping off his shirt as he ran. It only took him seconds to slip out of his tennis shoes and socks, then drop his shorts away from his swim trunks—seconds in which she glimpsed a tan, muscular body and a mass of brown hair on his chest. He dove into the water.

She hesitated, sitting to remove her shoes, lingering over the damp anklets.

"C'mon, the water'll fix you right up."

She stood up, feeling self-conscious again. Peeling off her wet shell and unwinding her tiny skirt seemed like a striptease—and he was watching her every move. Her bikini, worn so naturally on the beach, now seemed terribly skimpy.

"Irish lady, you just have to be the Old Sod's gift to America."

Despite herself she laughed, then dove into the pool. The water felt heavenly and it did renew her. She swam hard for a few moments, then rolled over into a backstroke. But her burst of energy was used up and, bone weary, she had to stand up. He was there.

"You're a good swimmer. Is there no end to your talents?"

She didn't know what to say. She knew only that the tops of her breasts floated just above the water line, and that this incredibly sexy man was standing only inches away from her, gazing unabashedly at her. Then Doris and Derek dove in. Geoff and Derek, always competitive, began to race the length of the pool, while Doris swam over in an easy side-stroke and joined her, wiping the water from her face with both hands. "Isn't he something?"

"I don't know. Is he?"

Doris laughed. "Don't give me that, Irish. You

didn't wear that itty-bitty bikini just to enter the Olympics."

At poolside Derek served tall, frosty vodka tonics. Irish stood, drying herself with a heavy beach towel, while Geoff stretched out on a recliner, letting the hot, late afternoon sun of August dry his body. There was a shining sleekness to him, rivulets coursing down his tanned body. He had a good build, broad shouldered, yet slender. He was lean and hard, without being excessively muscular. He obviously didn't go in for weightlifting, just plenty of exercise. He used his body for fun, rather than sculpted it out of vanity.

When he smiled at her, she looked away, accepting a drink from Derek, who was very different in appearance from his friend. Derek was shorter and far less handsome, with unruly brown hair and a mass of freckles. Doris always said he looked like Charlie Brown. It was hard to figure them as man and wife. He was so much more natural, easygoing, and unaffected than Doris. He had none of her bite. Yet they had been married a dozen years. Irish knew that as fond as she was of the witty Doris, she much preferred her husband's company.

Just then Doris deprived her of that, saying she needed him in the house and they went off, arms around each other. Irish knew it was just an excuse to leave her alone with Geoff. She didn't want that. She detested matchmakers. Having finished blotting the worst of the water from her hair, she draped the towel around her shoulders to cover her breasts.

"I make you ill at ease, don't I?"

Irish studied him. There was no smirking come-on in his face. It was just a simple, very direct question. "A little, yes," she said softly.

"I don't mean to. It's just that you're very beautiful and I enjoy looking at you."

She sat in a lawn chair opposite him, snugging the towel around her shoulders. "That doesn't help a bit."

"I'm sure it doesn't." He laughed. "Will it help if I say you make me ill at ease, too? You have an extraordinary way of looking at me. You're doing it right now. I feel like I have your complete attention. To have a beautiful woman look at me that way—" he smiled "—let's say I'm not used to it."

"I'm sorry." She wanted to look away from him, but couldn't actually avert her eyes from Geoff's face.

"Don't be. I'm certainly not." His smile faded and he became serious for a moment and then he laughed. He sat up in the recliner. "Doris tells me you're an illustrator—quite famous."

"Hardly. Illustrators are never famous—except for Norman Rockwell and Charles Dana Gibson. Our work is everywhere but hardly anyone knows who did it. I'm just fortunate to keep busy."

"Doing what?"

He seemed interested, so she told him. "A little of everything—book covers, record jackets, some ads, an occasional cereal box. I've illustrated some children's books. It doesn't pay well, but I enjoy it."

"Why do you call yourself an illustrator? Why not an artist or painter?"

"I have no pretense to art. An illustrator rarely seeks self-expression, rather tries to express the desires of a client. We are at best commercial artists, seeking to create that which pleases or meets the needs of persons who employ us."

"Doesn't every artist?"

"No, there's a big difference. A fine artist draws

or paints something that expresses himself or a concept. He then may sell his work to someone who appreciates it. An illustrator really reverses the process, creating what the buyer wants."

He looked at her intently. "I see what you mean —although I'm still willing to bet you are an artist."

She laughed. "No. Being able to draw does not make a person an artist."

He held up his hands in mock surrender. "All right, so you're an illustrator. What do you draw in, pen, charcoal, oils, or what?"

"All of them actually—whatever the customer wants or serves him best." Hesitantly at first, then in more detail as she became convinced of his interest, she described which medium was most appropriate to which type of illustration. "I guess I feel most at home in oils and use them whenever possible."

He smiled. "Like I say, you really are a painter. What are you working on now? I saw your smock covering your easel but didn't want to pry."

"Something very exciting, really." Her smile was quite radiant. "A major oil company has commissioned a series of magazine ads to honor women rulers—from Cleopatra to Margaret Thatcher. I'm doing the first group of them. It's quite a big job."

He was impressed. "A major oil company. I imagine that pays rather well."

"More than rather. It'll buy Sam a lot of dog food."

"The lucky dog." His broad smile easily became a laugh. "Congratulate him for me. All his years of struggle are finally paying off. I'm sure he deserves it."

"Yes, he does work hard." Her generous laugh

mingled with his. "Enough of me. What sort of law do you practice?"

"Nothing as interesting as you, I'm afraid. I do investment work—taxes, trusts, financial planning, that sort of thing. I guess I'm mostly a tax lawyer—telling people how to beat Uncle Sam."

"Are you in New York?"

"Yes. My office is on East Fifty-seventh. When you're in the city maybe we could meet for lunch or something."

"I just might do that. I need some help with my taxes and—" She saw him glance over her shoulder. She turned to see Doris and Derek returning. Both had showered and changed into matching pants and Hawaiian shirts, and he carried a tray of fresh drinks. Her first one was still untouched.

"So, have you two lovebirds gotten acquainted?"

Irish cringed inwardly. She swore Doris Parkins would say anything that came into her head. She certainly was the only one she knew who could get away with it.

Geoff seemed not to mind. "I have just learned the most fascinating information about illustrating. She was just telling me about a major ad campaign she's doing on women rulers." He turned to her. "Have you done any of them yet?"

"I'm just finished with the first—Queen Isabella of Spain." She smiled. "She was quite a lady. Spent ten years at war to drive the Moors from Spain. At the same time she ruled her country, sent Columbus off to discover America, *and* had several children."

Doris laughed. "Sounds like *my* marriage."

Derek was more serious. "Who're you doing next?"

"I'm not sure. I'm studying Cleopatra, but—"

"That ought to be sexy. I understand the fashions were very revealing in those days."

Irish made a face at Doris and so did her husband, who added, "Be serious." To Irish he said, "You were about to tell us something about Cleopatra."

Irish hesitated. She really didn't like to talk about her work or be the center of attention. "It was nothing, really."

"Yes, it was." Geoff leaned toward her. "I really am interested. What about Cleopatra?"

"She poses a problem, that's all. The idea of the ads is to capture the woman ruler at her moment of greatest triumph. It was easy with Isabella—the moment when Granada surrendered to her. With Elizabeth I of England it will be the defeat of the Spanish armada. With Cleopatra it is hard to decide. After all, she captivated both Julius Caesar and Marc Antony. Rome itself almost fell to her twice."

They discussed that for a while, with Derek arguing for Caesar and Geoff urging Marc Antony, while Doris, unable to suppress her wit, kept urging her to portray Cleopatra holding the asp against her breast. "That'll sell lots of oil," she said.

Irish shook her head at that, a gesture of mock exasperation over the hopelessness of her friend, and stood up. "All of which inspires me to get back to work. Thank you for—"

"You're not leaving. I won't hear of it." Doris seemed quite perturbed at her.

"I must. I have—"

"Nonsense. We've a few friends coming in—just cocktails and a little buffet. We need you."

"I'm sorry, I—"

"Geoff, talk some sense into her."

Irish didn't want to turn to him, but couldn't help

herself. She saw him urging her, his eyes pleading. She had to relent. There was no reason not to come, other than that she detested cocktail parties, but she'd look like a ninny if she said that. She forced a smile. "All right, but I still have to go home and change. I can hardly wear this swimsuit and towel."

Doris wouldn't let that go. "Why not, Irish? You'll be the hit of the party."

"I'm sure of that." Nervously she went to her tennis bag and began to stuff her shoes and whites inside. She hated driving home in her swimsuit, but she hated the thought of dressing in her soggy tennis attire even more. Why hadn't she thought to bring a change of clothing or a beach robe?

After "See you laters" and knowing looks from Doris, she and Geoff walked toward her car. She couldn't shake her self-consciousness and swore to God she'd go home and burn this bikini, never to wear it again.

He touched her arm, just above the elbow, a place that became instantly hot, hotter than the sun. She looked up at him.

"It'll be all right. I'll see that you have a good time."

She smiled, or tried to. "I'm just not wild about cocktail parties, that's all."

"Neither am I. But we'll manage together."

Together! The word stabbed at her. Here they were, both practically naked, his casual touch sending shock waves coursing through her body. *Together!* How long had it been for her?

They arrived at her car, a red MG with black leather upholstery. The top was down.

His eyes widened in admiration. "I love your wheels. Do you write it off?"

"What do you mean?"

His laugh was generous. "I should say you do need help with your taxes, but we'll see to that later." He opened the car door for her. "I understand how difficult cocktail parties must be for you, everyone jabbering at once, but I do appreciate your coming."

She stared at him. What did he mean?

"At least you'll know some of Doris's friends. I'll be a stranger."

It was an explanation. He didn't like crowds. Yes, that must be it. She slid into the car seat. It was hot from the sun and burned her bare thighs, but only for a moment. He closed the door carefully, dropped her tennis bag behind her seat, and leaned over her. She was sure he was going to kiss her.

"I'll pick you up at eight."

"You needn't do that. I can drive over."

"I know how independent you are." The combination of his nearness and his smile overpowered her. He had such a beautiful mouth. "But I'd really like to pick you up—just this once."

She stared at him, certain he would lean a little closer and kiss her now. "All right. I'll be ready." After the briefest of hesitations, she roared the car to life and sped off.

TWO

More than once she thought of begging off. She could go to Mrs. Harrington next door and ask her to phone and make some excuse for her. But no. She would just look stupid and Geoff would probably drive over and make her go.

Trouble was she did want to go, have fun, be with people—be with *him.* Aloud she said, "He's simply the most attractive man I've met in a long time, Sam. And he does seem interested in me—which I'm sure you find impossible to understand, you unromantic beast, you. But we have a problem, don't we?"

For the first time she felt the true legacy of Hank Peters. He had taught her just how much she needed companionship, affection, the rapture of being in love. He had seemed so right for her. But she wasn't right for him and could never be. Something she was powerless to change had ultimately destroyed their love. She just couldn't see herself going through it again with Geoff Winter or any other man.

"Sam, why don't you tell me to stop being such a ninny? Tell me to just go out for an evening, have a good time and let it go at that."

Yes. That's exactly what she'd do.

Irish had taken a long, hot shower and shampooed and dried her hair. Now she stood in a lacy bra and pantyhose over the bathroom sink finishing her eyes. She had applied the liner and just a hint of shadow and now brushed on the mascara which curled her naturally thick lashes. She surveyed the result. Her eyes were larger, their vivid blue accentuated. She made a face. Her eyes were probably too large to start with. She picked up her lipstick, then hesitated, studying the reflection in the mirror. He thought her beautiful. She shook her head and spoke aloud, "Well, you're not—hardly even a five. Your face is too oval and your mouth is definitely too small, the lips too full. You're just a weird-looking broad." In truth, she believed her self-appraisal unjust, but felt it necessary to avoid a big head. She glanced at her watch. Better hurry. Quickly she applied glossy lipstick to the mouth she thought was too small.

As she turned for the bedroom she almost tripped over Sam who was sprawled in the doorway. "I know you're a good watchdog, Sam, but you're overdoing it. You don't have to watch *everything* I do." His ears perked up at her words. Yes, Sam would look after her—better than anyone else. He seemed so friendly and affectionate, but she'd seen him when strangers came to the door, head down, fangs bared. She knew that with one word from her he'd turn into a tiger.

As she stepped over him into the bedroom, she said, "What'll I wear, love?" She already knew, but it was wise to at least let him think he was being consulted. Reaching into her closet, she said, "How about the blue silk shantung? You'll be crazy about it, Sam." It was one of her favorites, a two-piece suitdress, a shade of blue which nearly matched her eyes, simple, superbly tailored, and thereby very expensive. She stepped into and zipped up the thin, filmy skirt, cut narrow and very slimming. Then she slid her arms into the jacket. The feel of the fabric, cool, smooth, strangely sensuous, made her think of Geoff when he touched her.

She shook her head. *Stop it!* From a rack inside the closet door she selected a pair of matching, high-heeled blue slingbacks, just a couple of straps, very dainty, and sat on the edge of the bed to put them on. Sam raised his head, peering at her, head cocked to one side. "I'm like flash powder, Sam. One spark and I'll be gone. There is something about this man—or maybe it's me. He's just so darn appealing! If I'm not careful, I'll get into trouble. But I'll be *very* careful with Geoff Winter." She stood up, smoothing her skirt. "He's a gentleman, Sam, and I'm going to be very much a lady. I'll not let anything come between you and me again. Once burned is—" She laughed lightly. "Something once burned is thrown into the rubbish."

She had just finished dabbing on a bit of *Je Reviens* when Sam bolted for the door. Geoff was standing there looking excruciatingly handsome in gray slacks, a yellow shirt, open at the throat, a navy blue blazer, and loafers. He looked casual yet elegant, as if everything he was wearing had been tailored especially for him. Bending down to pat Sam, he smiled up at her. "I think I'd better learn some new adjectives."

She laughed. "I guess this dress is a little more attractive than a soggy sweat suit."

"I know beautiful women don't like to be raved over—on the theory everybody has some kind of looks and it isn't important—but, Irish lady, you are a vision."

She felt color rising in her cheeks and tried to fight it. "You're just partial to Irish coloring."

"On you at least."

She was grateful another rejoinder came to her. "I'll accept the compliment—and try to introduce you to some other Irish lasses." She hesitated, uncertain what to say next. "Shall we go? Or would you like a drink first?"

"A drink—Scotch if you have it, with a splash of water. I'd hoped to see some of your work."

She motioned toward the easel and went into the kitchen to make his drink and pour a little Chablis for herself. When she returned he was looking intently at her painting. "I'm no critic, Irish, but—"

She wanted to keep it light and interrupted. "Thank God for that."

He looked at her. "I think it's wonderful. You've certainly portrayed Granada. Ever been there?"

"No. I wish I had. I was forced to use photographs, other drawings."

"No one would ever know it." He turned back to her painting. "That's Granada, not just today but as it must have looked then. You can see the city from a long distance. It's breathtaking."

"Thank you, sir. You earned a drink." She handed it to him.

He accepted, but idly, continuing to focus on the painting. "I'm amazed at your talent. Look what's in Isabella's face—triumph, joy, pride, yet there is a womanly quality to her. It is almost as though she's sorry. She understands how the Moor feels."

Irish sucked in her breath with an audible sound. He had expressed precisely what she had tried to put into the painting.

"How can you do that—express all that emotion in her face?"

"I—I don't know." She was surprised by his question, the depth of understanding it suggested. "I read all I could about her." She gestured toward books scattered about the room. "I tried to understand how she felt—put myself inside her skin. I just . . . drew. I guess the hand expressed what I felt."

He smiled. "And you say you're not an artist."

Her laugh was nervous. "Not that again."

His attention returned to the painting. "The caliph doesn't look too happy."

"I'm sure he wasn't. He really did cry, but I took a small liberty with the facts. He actually turned the keys to Granada over to King Ferdinand." She pointed. "That's him standing a little behind Isabella. No Moslem could be expected to surrender to a woman. I thought—"

"Of course. This is about women rulers. Can't have Ferdinand stealing the glory." He was silent a moment, studying the painting, then he was smiling at her. "I think it's splendid, Irish. The ad campaign just has to be successful. Women will love it—men, too."

She looked into his eyes, so intense, drawing her to him. Softly she said, "Let's hope all men are like you."

"We're not so bad—if given a chance. We're learning. You're a talented, accomplished, independent woman. I find that very attractive."

She laughed lightly. "And all the while I thought it was my Irish coloring."

"It doesn't hurt any." He took a generous swallow from his drink. "Is there anything else I can look at?"

"I've some rough sketches for other paintings in the series. Would you like to see those?" He did and for the next several minutes she showed him her drawings, explaining what she planned to do with the finished painting. He was extremely interested and asked many questions. Finally she asked, "Are you sure you're a lawyer and not an art director?"

He laughed. "I neither draw nor paint. In fact I'm lucky I can write my name. But that doesn't mean I can't appreciate talent."

"You certainly are appreciative. I just wish art directors were half as appreciative as you." She set down her mostly untouched glass of wine. "Hadn't we better be going? Doris will get wild ideas about what we're up to."

"Not yet." He handed her his glass. "I'll swap another one of these for some free advice on your taxes. You said you need help. What do you do, just pay them?"

"Doesn't everyone?"

"Not one penny more than they have to. It's my job to see they don't."

She was in the kitchen now, making his drink. In a moment she brought it to him and motioned for him to sit on the couch. She then retrieved her wine and sat in an overstuffed chair by the fireplace.

"Do you have an accountant?"

She sighed and shook her head. "I know I should, but—" She shrugged, a gesture of futility. "For a long time I didn't make much money and an accountant seemed an expense. Later, I just never found the time."

"Who does your taxes?"

"I just get everything together and send it to the IRS office."

He shook his head and let out his breath in a distinct "Whew" sound. "That's foolish, Irish. It's all right for a wage earner, but you operate a business. You have to—"

"A business?"

"Yes, the business of illustrating. And you have a

cost of doing business—paint, canvas, brushes, other supplies. You buy books, magazines, postage." He made an expansive gesture to encompass the whole room. "This house is your place of business. Some portion of it—at least half, I guess—should be written off as a business expense."

"You mean I can deduct half my rent?"

"And your utilities. You have to be warm in winter and have light in which to work. Your car is partly an expense. I'm sure you at least drive it to the post office." He smiled. "As a matter of fact, you can write off the cost of these two drinks I've had as an entertainment expense. We're discussing your taxes."

She laughed. "I can't really do that?"

He was serious. "Yes, you can—and you'd better. It's perfectly legal."

She sipped her wine and studied him over the rim of the glass. "I guess I've been rather silly, haven't I?"

"Yes, but it may not be too late. If you'll let me have your tax forms for the last few years, I'll study them. We may be able to approach IRS about overpayment of your taxes and get you a refund. I can't promise it will work, but we can try."

She rose and went to a filing cabinet in the corner behind her easel. Opening it, she said, "I'm really more organized than you might think." In a moment she handed him a folder containing her accumulated tax forms.

"Give me a few days and I'll get back to you."

"Do I really get all this for a drink?"

"It was an awfully good one."

The party was as she feared. Doris's "few friends" turned out to be more than twenty couples, creating a nightmarish situation for Irish. She was best one-to-one. She could handle two or three people, but a half dozen around her, all talking at once, was a fragmented kaleidoscope. She caught only an occasional word or two and everything said was meaningless.

Geoff tried to stay with her, but Doris kept leading him away like her proud possession to be shown off to somebody new. Irish did her best to mingle, her face frozen into a smile, hoping her nods and laughs and "I declares" and other noncommittal expressions were appropriate and well-timed. The truth was she was exhausted, depressed, her nerves taut and jangling.

She was sustained by Geoff, who kept catching her eye across the room. Then he was at her side. "You look beat. Have you eaten all day?"

She tried to think. Orange juice was all she could remember. "I just need some air. It's the smoke, I think."

"All right, air first, then food." He led her outside to the patio, then across the lawn toward the pool and tennis court.

She took in gulps of air, fragrant with flowers. She didn't recognize any of the scents and promised herself to learn more about flowers. Then she looked up at a turquoise sky against a nearly full moon, partially hidden behind the shade of tall trees. "A heavenly night," she whispered, "bewitching."

He took her hand, gently, companionably, as though she were a child, and led her up the sloping lawn toward the pool. She felt her heels digging into the wet grass. They rounded a tree branch low to the ground—maple, she thought—then were at the fence surrounding the pool. He unlatched the

31

gate and they stood on the deck where they had been in the afternoon. They were away from the trees now, bathed in moonlight. She saw the silvery reflection undulating on the surface of the water, then looked skyward. "A magical night."

With gentle pressure of his fingers against her hand, he turned her to face him. "No," he whispered, "you are the magic." Then his free hand touched her chin, raising it, and he kissed her.

She saw it coming and welcomed it. His lips were soft, the kiss gentle. But she gasped as delicious sensations swept through her, blowing away the ashes of longing igniting a small spark of desire into a dangerous conflagration of passion.

He swept her into his arms, pressing her forcefully against him as he claimed her mouth, more roughly this time. She felt the tension that had been with her all day ooze out of her, and she gave herself up to him as his lips, open now, moved against hers, exploring and stoking hot desires within her. When his tongue entered her mouth she shivered under an onslaught of pleasure. Then he was at her ear, nibbling gently. Moving lower, his lips brushed across the side of her neck, before returning to her mouth, creating ravenous hungers. She gasped anew, feeling the sensitive tips of her breasts pressing against his chest, knowing she was so overwhelmed by this man she wouldn't be standing if it weren't for his strong arms clasping her against him.

"Oh, please," she moaned, feeling the heat and pulsating hardness of him.

She was trembling, quivering all over with the sweet sensations Geoff was provoking in her.

At its end she knew he was speaking, but she couldn't follow, couldn't concentrate. She felt disoriented, dizzy, and knew only that he was turning her, his arm around her shoulders, leading her back to the party.

They sat on a swinging divan on the patio, another couple nearby. She could see him clearly now in the better light. He was smiling when he spoke. "I knew it would be like that." She nodded. There was nothing to say. "All day long I knew it would be like that. May I say it was hell waiting?" He smiled again. "But worth it."

She felt he had bared her soul, unlocking the secret passions she alone knew were within her. He had no right. She didn't know if she wanted to share these feelings with him.

They went inside and mingled with the others. She tried to clear her head. He had kissed her, that was all. So he had discovered how passionate she was, how starved. It need not lead to more. She could handle him now.

He was at her side. "Let's get out of here."

She nodded. Yes. She was exhausted. She wanted to go home, to Sam, her secure, orderly life. She needed to think.

They rode to her house in silence. He stopped in front and helped her out, then took her hand and led her through the carport, past the MG to the beach in back to watch the moonlight on the surf and a few frolicking bathers. He held only her hand, leading her back to the cottage. It was on the darkened porch that he kissed her.

She was powerless against her own nature. On tiptoes now, she felt almost swept off her feet, with her body pressed against his, and her hands caressing the back of his neck. Hungry for her sweetness, his tongue darted into her mouth, teasing her, caressing her. Their breathing was hot and ragged.

They needed more air, but could not release each other to find it.

She felt his hand on her bare back, under her jacket, stroking her mercilessly, arousing hot, tingling sensations in her breasts and thighs. She wanted him, but knew she couldn't have him.

"No more, Geoff, please." She pushed at his arms and was free of him. She knew he was saying something, but she could think only of getting inside the cottage where she'd be safe from him—and herself.

He took the key from her and unlocked the door. When he stood back for her to enter, she quickly shut the screen door. "I'm sorry, Geoff. It was a lovely evening, but-but I'm really tired. I'm not ready for. . . ."

She saw his face pressed against the screen, picking up the interior light. She saw his moving lips and read them. "I just want to talk, Irish, but I can't out here. It's dark and you can't see what I'm saying."

She stared at him in disbelief. "You know?"

"Yes, I've known all day."

THREE

"You have to be the best lip-reader in the world. Once or twice I was almost convinced I was wrong about your being deaf. Can you hear nothing?"

She had let him inside, too stunned to be aware of her actions. Even now she could only shake her head. Remembered speech, much practiced, had fled her.

"It must be very difficult for you."

For a moment she stared at him, then slowly closed her eyes, blotting out both him and his words, bringing darkness to her silent world. Of all men, this one, so attractive, so desirable, knew her secret. Then she looked at him. Her voice was sad, weary as she asked, "How did you know I was deaf? Did Doris tell you?"

"No, I don't think she knows. She never mentioned it if she does."

"Then how?"

"Does it matter? Believe me, knowing you're deaf hasn't bothered me all day. It doesn't now." His smile was soft, full of understanding.

"I asked how you knew." She had read only condescension in his words. Her anger rose and her voice took on a sharp edge. "I have a right to know."

Concern for her showed in his face. "It wasn't difficult. Your lack of a phone for starters. That is strange in a place like Westport. Then Sam gave you away. He was making an ungodly racket at the door. You didn't silence him because you didn't hear him. And there were times I spoke to you and you didn't reply. Once or twice I deliberately turned my back. I realized you were lipreading, not hearing."

She shook her head in despair, and a sound of anguish came from her. Her tone was brittle as she said, "I'm going to get a damn phone tomorrow. When I don't answer I'll tell people I was out." She turned to her dog. "Sam, help me remember to stop your yapping."

He touched her shoulder, turning her back to him. "Why are you angry?"

"Why shouldn't I be angry? You've no idea how hard I've worked to conceal my handicap. Then I meet some . . . some know-it-all and he spots me right away."

"Most people probably don't." He grinned. "But then I was especially interested in you."

"*I wish you weren't,*" she said emphatically, then wheeled and stalked to the fireplace, leaning over it, hands on the mantel, looking down, trying to control her anger. Finally she was able to breathe normally and turned to face him. With excessive politeness she said, "Would you mind leaving, Geoff? It's been a long day. I'm exhausted." As if to prove it she plopped into the stuffed chair by the fireplace.

"I should imagine you are. That party must have been hell for you—everyone talking at once, some half drunk, slurring their speech, others with their mouths full of food."

She rested her head against the back of the chair and closed her eyes, emotional and physical weariness weighing on her. She felt dizzy, disoriented, too tired even to be angry. She sighed, then said, her voice soft, "I have the most trouble with tight-

36

lipped people who speak at the back of their mouths. You see them a lot in New England." She forced her eyes open for his reply.

"I know the type—finishing school grads. They talk in a monotone."

"I wouldn't know what they sound like." Again she closed her eyes. "Please leave now. I mean it when I say I'm exhausted." Alone in her silent world, she felt herself sinking into unconsciousness. It felt heavenly. But it was not to be. She felt him sit on the arm of the chair, intruding on her privacy. She opened her eyes to protest.

He was shaking his head. "I won't leave you like this, Irish. I have to know why it matters so much if people know you're deaf."

"Why? That's a stupid question." Again her anger rose, but this time she tamped it down quickly. "I'm sorry. I guess you couldn't be expected to know. Few people have any idea what it's like to be handicapped in America. We put such a premium on physical perfection, on the body beautiful that we discriminate—without even realizing it—against anyone who isn't: the deaf, blind, lame, anyone who speaks peculiarly, the scarred. Heavens, it's a handicap simply to grow old and have wrinkles in America."

"You exaggerate."

"I do not. Did you know a group of travelers were refused admittance to a major-chain hotel in Mississippi simply because they were deaf? Airlines insist on taking blind people aboard airplanes in wheelchairs, apparently because they think the blind can't walk. They are forced to sit at the bulkhead lest they upset or maybe *contaminate* the other passengers. *Then* they are made to sit on blankets on the assumption that being blind makes one incontinent."

She saw his surprise. "There are 32 million handicapped people in the United States. If you don't believe me, ask any one of them."

"Okay, but—"

"There are no buts, Geoff. I've lived through it. As soon as people know I'm deaf, the first thing they do is shout. I can see them doing it. They can holler their lungs out, they can set off an atomic bomb, and I still won't hear them. Or, they start speaking pidgin English and making lots of gestures, as though I'm a foreigner and don't understand the language. Then there are their eyes. They are uncomfortable, guilty, grateful it isn't them. They don't know what to say or how to act—except that they ought to treat me somehow *differently*. They turn away from that which is strange and pitiful and ugly. Or worse they offer only condescension—or treat you like you are *totally* helpless. Can you imagine what it's like to be stopped by a cop? If he finds out I'm deaf, the first thing he does is try to haul me in on the theory the deaf have no right to drive. Then he hunts up someone who knows sign. He won't believe I can understand him. And all that is just the tip of the iceberg. I haven't even mentioned the problems of insurance, banking, or housing."

He stared at her, wide-eyed, as though in shock. "I never thought of all that. Do you really have this trouble?"

"Yes—or I used to. I'm luckier than most. I was twelve when I went deaf. I have memory of speech and I go to therapy to maintain it. But I had a hard time learning to lip-read. I never thought I'd learn. It took me years."

"You're marvelous at it now."

"I hope so. All I know is that I just had to learn. I

38

wasn't going to wear a sign around my neck saying I was deaf. I wanted to be treated like everyone else. I wanted a career and independence and a normal life. I wanted. . . ." She sighed, then let her head fall back against the chair. "Why did you have to spot me right away and spoil everything."

She closed her eyes, dejected, bone weary now and close to tears. But in a moment she felt his finger touch her cheek, beckoning her to open her eyes, not close him out. "Thank you. I understand now why you conceal your deafness. Does it help if I say you're very good at it? I doubt if most people suspect it."

She stared at him through teary blue eyes. He was swimming in her vision, yet she saw the tenderness, the sincerity in his face.

"I have just one question, Irish. Have I treated you any differently today? I said you were a beautiful, accomplished, and independent woman—highly attractive to me. I mean it—more than ever now that I know the truth."

What a thing to say! Tears rolled down her cheeks. She was unable to halt the flow or diminish the ache in her throat.

"Have you no family?"

She shook her head slowly several times. "My—my parents . . . and sister—" she swallowed "—were killed in a . . . plane crash—" a sign now "—shortly after I went deaf." She could not hear how strained her voice was.

"What caused your deafness?"

Another difficult swallow. "Spinal . . . meningitis. I was twelve. My family was . . . k-killed . . . when I was in . . . deaf school."

"God!" The word burst from him. "How alone you must be."

"I'm fine. I get along . . . just fine."

He stared at her a long moment. "I've been thinking about you all day, wondering what it must be like to be deaf. For the first time I became aware of the sounds I take for granted—that ticking clock, its chimes, the refrigerator humming, Sam licking his chops just now. You don't hear the surf out there, the laughter from the beach, the traffic noises, or rain, wind, and leaves." He shook his head. "For heaven's sake, the sound of another human voice. You must feel very isolated."

She trembled, couldn't help it. Why did he have to know all that? "I—I don't mind. I—I have the memory of it all. It pleases me." She glanced up at the mantel. "I remember my mother's clock chiming. I look at the hour and know that it is. It does still chime, doesn't it?"

"Yes, beautifully." Again he shook his head, as though trying to deny his new awareness. "What do you miss the most?"

"Music. I loved music."

"You can't even play the radio! I forgot that." Agitated, he stood up, took a couple of steps away from her, wheeled. "I don't think I could stand being so alone."

He knew too much. He was invading her private world. "I'm used to it. I get along just fine."

"I doubt that. Everyone needs someone."

Why wouldn't he leave her alone? "I have my friends . . . Sam. He's trained as a hearing dog. He alerts me to bells, horns, sirens, warning noises I can't hear. He's my protector." It seemed to her his head was moving, beginning to whirl, fading a little in her vision. She was so tired. All this . . . too much. "I have my work. I'm . . . very busy.

I—" She forced her drooping lids open. "I've made my own way."

"Look, Irish. I was kissed tonight by someone in great need. You were on fire, reaching out for someone to put out those flames. I've never known such passion as yours. You are very attracted to me. You can't deny it."

Concentrating on his moving lips seemed to sap all her strength and she closed her eyes. All she wanted to do was sleep. Why wouldn't he go, leave her alone? She struggled to stay awake. *You can't deny it.* What was it she couldn't deny? she wondered sleepily. She'd think of it in a minute. . . .

The smell of frying bacon was pungent, filling the whole house. It must be Sunday. Her father always cooked Sunday breakfast, enough for an army, bacon, sausage, eggs, home fries—pancakes, too, with real maple syrup. She would jump out of bed and run downstairs in her flannel nightgown for Daddy to sweep her into his arms, hug her, call her "punkin."

Bacon. She opened her eyes. She was in her own bedroom, yet there it was, the smell of bacon. Wide-eyed with shock, she remembered. Geoff had been here. Bacon! He must *still* be here.

Frantic, she raised the sheet and light blanket and looked down at herself. She still wore the blue silk shantung and stockings. Her shoes were gone. He had put her to bed! He didn't *dare!*

In one movement Irish sat up, twisted her feet off the bed, and stood up. Then she looked down at herself. Her suit was shamelessly wrinkled. Couldn't be seen this way. Checking to see that the door was closed, she quickly stripped off the jacket and stepped out of the skirt, reaching for her white

41

terry cloth robe. Then she hesitated, stripping off her stockings, her bra, too, and wrapped her nakedness in the heavy robe, cinching the belt tightly.

Opening the door, she saw the couch, pillows stacked at one end, a blanket tossed carelessly aside. He had slept here. She took two steps and turned toward the kitchen.

She was angry. After all, he had slept in her house uninvited, but what she saw made her smile. He was in his shirt-sleeves, spatula in hand, hovering over the stove. His blond hair was tousled and one of her dainty aprons was tied to his waist. Sam was sitting at his feet, hoping for a handout. It was a scene so domestic she had to laugh.

When he turned she saw he had been whistling. Now concern showed in his eyes. "Are you all right?"

"I'm fine. What did I do, fall asleep?"

"Yes—in the chair. I couldn't leave you there so I carried you into the bedroom. I was going to lock up and leave, then I remembered you didn't eat at the party. Thought I'd hang around and look after you. Hope you don't mind." Then he grinned. "That wasn't exactly the way I hoped to get you into bed."

She shook her head at him. "I'm sure I'll never convince Doris all I had was a good night's sleep."

"I thought about that but figured I'm a big boy and you're a big girl and we don't have to make explanations."

"I hope you're right." She smiled. "That bacon smells heavenly."

His eyes widened. "The bacon! It'll be burned to a crisp." He turned and jerked the frying pan off the burner.

Ten minutes later they sat on the two stools at the

counter, digging into heaping plates of scrambled eggs, English muffins and well-done bacon. Almost at once she felt her vigor return. "You're a good cook," she said through a mouthful of food.

"That's because you're starved. Do you always forget to eat—or are you anorexic?"

"I eat. In fact, I love to cook. Yesterday was an unusual day, that's all."

He smiled. "You can say that again."

"Yesterday was an unusual day." Her laugh almost made her splatter food on him and she had to cover her mouth with her hand.

They ate in silence then, but as starved as she had been, she quickly became full, pushing the plate away, wiping her lips. "You can have the rest if you want."

He leisurely placed his fork on the side of his plate and wiped his lips. "I've had plenty, thanks. That's not what I want anyway." He turned to her, eyes smoldering.

She did not oppose the kiss. It was soft, gentle, his slightly open lips enveloping her smaller mouth, testing for fullness, finding pillowy softness. It was different from the hungry, urgent kisses they'd shared in the moonlight, but still it bespoke their desire for each other.

He pulled away and when she saw his lips move she knew his voice was low, husky. "Would you like to try for another unusual day?"

He was all mouth to her—and beckoning eyes. "I can't. I work seven days a week. I have to—to keep up."

"All right, this evening. We could—"

She shook her head gently.

"You know you want to."

He leaned toward her again, and again she

couldn't resist his kiss, which was deeper now, more urgent, electric with sensation, propelling desires into her. Nor could she resist his touch when his hand slipped inside her robe and found her breasts, caressing them, kneading them gently. When his thumb began to stroke one of her nipples, she shuddered as exquisite sensations skittered over the length of her body. His tongue found hers, smooth, sweet, and she moaned her satisfaction.

"You know you want to," Geoff repeated huskily, "you're on fire again."

"Yes, I want you—and I am on fire." She made no effort to remove his cupping hand or stop the revolving motions of his thumb. "But it is a fire which will just have to burn—" she smiled, or tried to "—like that coal mine in Pennsylvania nobody can put out."

He squeezed her breast, intensifying the motions of his thumb, driving her mad with desire for him. "Your skin is so soft. I feel like my hand is immersed in down."

"Thank you." She could barely utter the words. But when his lips again came toward her, she turned away. "You're just making it harder, Geoff— for both of us."

He looked at her a long moment, as though plumbing the depths of her eyes in search of some secret. Then he slumped back against the stool, removing his hand from her. Suddenly she felt deprived.

"Can you tell me why? Is it because you're deaf?"

She pursed her lips, looking at him. She felt so sad. "Maybe, I suppose so. I just know it will never work. I could take you into the bedroom and let you love me and love me and love me, as I would love you back. It's all I want to do. But then what? Is there an encore other than pain and loss and greater loneliness?"

"There could be."

She slid off the stool, tightening her robe, and on bare feet walked over to her drawing board, standing over it, placing a poster card in a position for her to begin to fill it. "I really do work hard—particularly the next few days. I took too long with the Isabella painting. I'm overdue on a book jacket. I have to catch up."

He was beside her now, his arm around her shoulder, his hand turning her chin so she had to look at him, see what he wanted to say. "I work hard, too. You have no monopoly on hard work, Irish."

She nodded. "I didn't mean to suggest that." She twisted away from him and went to sit on the arm of the chintz chair by the fireplace so she could face him. Her robe fell open, revealing a snowy calf and thigh. She was unaware of it. "I tried once, Geoff. His name was Hank, Hank Peters. Ran a local camera shop. Also sold art supplies. I used to go in, make purchases." She sighed. "One thing led to another. You know how that goes."

His vivid blue eyes seemed to bore into her. She looked away, down at herself, adjusted the open robe, then began to twist the end of the belt. "He wasn't as handsome as you." She hesitated and smiled sadly. This was all so hard to say, but she had to. "He moved in here. Sam was just a puppy then. My career was just taking off. It was an exciting time for me. I thought I had everything." She shrugged. "I didn't."

She looked up, saw him say, "What went wrong?"

Her smile was wan, sardonic. "You know how it is. A man wants attention, lots of attention sometimes. I was busy with my work, very involved, concentrating hard, but I tried." She sighed. "It wasn't enough. He'd speak to me from the bathroom or bedroom, the porch, someplace, and I wouldn't hear him. He thought I was ignoring him. It made him angry. The fights got worse. We parted—not entirely amicably."

"You didn't tell him you were deaf?"

"Not at first."

"You should have. You owed it to him."

She nodded her head slowly. "I suppose. I intended to every day, but we were so happy. It didn't seem necessary. Then one day he screamed at me, 'Are you deaf or something?' I told him that's exactly what I was." She looked down at her hands. "That's when the real problems began. I'd just as soon not go into all that, if you don't mind."

Geoff went to her, taking both her hands, making her look at him. "I already know you're deaf, Irish. It wouldn't bother me."

"There was another thing. You read in books about lovemaking, how the man makes little sounds, sighs, moans of pleasure, whispers love words. I can't hear those sounds and I can't keep my eyes open to read his lips. Maybe it's dark. As much as I enjoyed it, I decided lovemaking was a solitary exercise, just me, my pleasure. I began to feel excruciatingly alone, more alone than at any other time."

He moved away from her, back to the counter, picking up his cup of cold coffee, drinking from it nonetheless. She watched him. "Everybody closes their eyes when they make love, Irish. Both partners are alone, contained within themselves. That's the mystery of it. Two solitary people join together in a shared act of love. Neither can ever know, no matter how hard they try to describe it, exactly what the other is feeling." He smiled. "So they try again and again, keeping on trying their whole lives, hoping to solve the mystery."

She smiled radiantly. "I said you were a poet." But her smile quickly faded. "It'll just never work, Geoff—for us. As much as I want you—and believe me I do want you, more than you know—I don't want to get involved with you. I can't stand the pain of parting—and there will be a parting, believe me. I had a hard time after Hank left. The loneliness was . . . very difficult. My work suffered. I got behind. I can't afford to let that happen again." She sighed. "But I got over it. Sam and I have built a good life here. I don't need anyone." She tried to smile, but it was not very successful. "I'm sorry, Geoff, but I have to protect myself—and my career."

He tried to pick up the cup of coffee again, but his hand was shaking too much.

"Are you angry?"

"A little—and trying not to be. I think you're being most unfair. For starters, I'm not—"

"Would you face me? It's hard to read lips when you're sideways."

"I'm sorry. I forgot." When he turned she saw the hard glint of anger in his eyes, the firmness of his mouth. "I said you're wrong on several counts. First, I'm Geoff Winter, not Hank whatshisname. I don't even know the man. Second, who said anything about moving in here? I have my own place in Manhattan. I plan to keep it. Third, I'm not about to interfere with your work. I admire it. I was only suggesting we go out to dinner tonight."

She could not hear but nonetheless felt the coldness in his voice. His eyes left no doubt of it. But she stood up to it. "I'm sorry. I guess I'm being forward. Or am I? As you say, I'm a big girl and you're a big boy. I want you and you want me. We both know what will happen after dinner."

"Maybe. What if it does?"

She pressed her lips hard together. "There are some beginnings best never made, Geoff. It will be wonderful at first—I'm sure of that—but it will soon fall apart." She saw him trying to speak and raised her hand to stop him. "I'm not a sprinter in the relays of love, Geoff. I'm a marathon woman, trained for the long run, a lifetime run."

"How do you know I'm not?"

"I don't, of course."

"How do you know I'm not looking for the right woman to love, marry, share my life with?"

She inhaled deeply and tears welled into her eyes unbidden. "Geoff, don't you think I sense what a good man you are? I wouldn't be talking like this if I didn't think you were."

"Then what are you trying to say?"

She shook her head in frustration, then wiped away a tear under her eye with her fingertips. "You just don't know. You'll try and I'll try, but it'll just never work. There'll be novelty at first, but that will soon wear off. In the beginning we'll be in love and happy, but the problems will emerge and destroy both. I'm not prepared to cope with that. I doubt if you are either."

"Are you talking about your deafness?"

"You have no idea of the difficulties involved in a relationship between a hearing and nonhearing person. I do. I've been there."

"Hank again. I told you I'm not him."

She knew he'd raised his voice, and she did too. "I know you're different, but the problems remain the same."

"Name one."

"All right, I'll start you off with an easy one. I read your lips. I think, believe, hope I'm catching every word you utter. But I have to concentrate. Suppose I'm distracted. Suppose I miss a word like a *no* or *not* and completely misunderstand what you've said. How are you going to react?"

"That hasn't happened."

"Hasn't it? I only *think* I know what you've said. The simple truth is that I guess a lot. I may be dead wrong. Want some more? Remember, I only read lips. The words are very literal to me. I don't hear the inflection in your voice. You may be kidding or facetious or sarcastic or just plain mean. If you speak with a poker face I can't tell the difference. Half the time I'm not sure whether Doris is kidding or not. Believe me, Geoff, all this is just for starters —to use your expression."

His mouth opened, then closed. He had nothing to say, but she knew his silence didn't mean he was convinced. "Geoff, speech is equated with intelligence in our society. A person who talks imperfectly or misunderstands a lot or doesn't catch on to a joke is thought to be slow, not very smart, even stupid. Sooner or later, after the umpteenth time I don't catch on to something and you have to explain it, you'll begin to wonder if I'm as smart as you once thought. You know the expression—deaf and dumb."

She watched him stride to a chair, snatch his jacket from the back, and put it on. "Are you angry with me?"

He turned to her. "No, not angry—saddened I guess, maybe a little hurt. Look, I like you a lot. We've just met but for some reason I care about you

49

and want to get to know you better. But you won't even give me a chance."

Irish looked up into his blue eyes. *Oh, dear God*, she thought, *he is such a magnificent man—so strong and caring and tender. Just the sort of man I'd like to have a future with.* "I want to," she said, swallowing hard. "God, how much I want to believe it would work with you—with us. It's just—"

"I know. You needn't explain anymore." He reached down and patted the dog. "At least Sam and I get along."

She watched him head for the door. "Geoff?" He turned to her. "I'm sorry. I feel so *awful*."

"I know. I do too."

Then he was gone.

FOUR

Eyes wide, mouth open, she stared at the door, as though it were capable of recalling the man who had just passed through it. She wanted to run after him. *Geoff, come back! I didn't mean it. Please stay.* But her feet had turned to stone. She blinked once, twice, then closed her eyes, hoping to blot out the emptiness. *Irish!* The sound of her name startled her and she ran to the door, expectant. After his car was gone, she shook her head. False hearing. It happened sometimes, the memory of speech playing tricks on her mind.

Dejected, utterly desolate, the silence of her world so penetrating it was painful, she slowly turned away from the door. She felt like a void, drained, empty, a vacuum. Her familiar room was now foreign. Then she saw Sam, standing by the counter, wagging his tail, looking at her beseechingly. He was real. She knew what he wanted.

Slowly she went to the kitchen, scraping the cold eggs, bacon, and muffins, quite a lot really, into Sam's bowl, watching him gulp it down, then lap water. "I know you think I'm an idiot, Sam, but I know I'm right. It never would have worked. As bad as I feel now, think how much worse it would be if—if we'd really done anything." She pulled her robe tighter around herself, as though hiding the breast he had touched. "We're better off without him,

51

Sam, much better off—and so is he. It never would have worked."

She began to clean up the breakfast dishes, filling the sink with sudsy water, dropping plates and cups into it. On her second trip to the counter she saw his apron, her apron really, draped over the back of a stool. In her inner vision he was wearing it. *You won't even give me a chance.* "I did so, Sam. You notice he didn't put up much of an argument. He did sort of skulk out without a fight, didn't he? Probably very glad to be rid of us." Yes. She put the apron away out of sight, then began to wash the dishes, leaving them to drain on the counter.

None of this was normal for her. Usually she arose, dressed, drank orange juice, and went right to work. Dishes and housekeeping were usually done late at night and sometimes not for two or three days at a time. But just now dishes and tidying up were important acts. She was regrouping, she knew, picking up the pieces of her life, hoping to glue them back together.

Dishes done, she went into the main room and saw his blanket on the couch. *Everyone needs someone.* She shook her head. "Will you stop it? For crying out loud, he's just a guy you met, played tennis with, and smooched a couple of times in the moonlight. He wasn't exactly Paul Newman." She went to the couch, fluffed the pillows he had used, then folded the blanket and put it away. Was that the last of him? She scanned the room for more evidence. There was none.

"Time to get to work, Irish." Yes. Resolved now, she marched into the bedroom, made the bed, put last night's shoes away, folded the silk shantung to go to the cleaners. In the bathroom she rinsed out her pantyhose and undergarments, hanging them up to dry. Back in the bedroom she stripped off her robe to dress, then glimpsed her nakedness in the mirror. *I've never known such passion as yours. You can't deny it.* Angrily she said, "Who's denying it? Sure, I'm a very sexy dame." She saw Sam in the doorway, ears cocked, head sideways, listening. "So he's a good kisser. You can find one on every street corner." Yes, anger helped. It felt better than the emptiness.

Quickly she donned a sleeveless blouse and jeans and went to her drawing board, determined to work and forget Geoff Winter. The book jacket she was to do was for a paperback spy novel, known in publishing as a thriller. She had read every word of it so as to make the cover as accurate as possible. It was a point of pride with her, for she knew not all illustrators bothered. The book was steamy, with a James Bond–type hero bedding a succession of improbable lovelies. As she began to sketch she said, "Just what I need to work on today, Sam." Her sarcasm was lost on her dog.

The scene she wanted to portray on the jacket was of a startled, very disappointed hero being confronted by a sexy woman holding a gun on him. Shouldn't be hard. With a pencil she began to trace in the figures, hero in the foreground, femme fatale further back. *And you say you're not an artist.* "So he likes my work. Lots of people do. It's how I earn my living."

A half hour later she threw her pencil down in disgust. The face she had just sketched on the hero was unmistakably that of Geoff Winter. Angrily she said, "You noticed, Sam, how he arranged it so I'd feel guilty. 'All I wanted to do was take you out to dinner,' he said. 'You never gave me a chance.' He must really think I was born yesterday." Much too vigorously she erased the face and tried again. Another likeness of Geoff Winter appeared beneath her hand.

More slowly now she put the pencil aside. "I suppose I should have done it differently, Sam. He is a nice man. I could have gone out with him, explained better, kept him as a friend." She shook her head several times. "No, it never would have worked. As was proved last night and this morning, he and I can't be in the same room for more than five minutes without having to touch each other." A vision of what it might be like to touch Geoff Winter in the most intimate way in bed flittered across her mind. Shocked at herself, she stood up. "I know I'm right, Sam. It's better this way."

It became a wasted day. She ran with Sam until she was ready to drop, took a long swim, then lay in the sun, hoping to fall asleep. That was a mistake, for the hot rays of the sun were as his touch and behind closed eyelids his kisses were . . . She jumped up, ran into the house. Had to keep busy. Work was impossible, so she pampered herself; a long shower, shampoo, finishing off with stinging cold water. She did everything she could think of, a wax job on her legs and underarms, plucked her eyebrows, trimmed a little off her hair, gave herself a meticulous manicure and pedicure—three coats —and she seldom wore nail polish.

The clock was an enemy, time something to be filled. She took Sam and drove to the cleaners, then stopped at the Laundromat—two loads. Next she shopped, oh so carefully, for groceries she really didn't need, came home and began to prepare the most elaborate meal she could think of, *coq au vin*.

About six, just as she was ready to put on the rice Doris Parkins came. She wore a fetching chartreuse pantsuit and was in rare form. "What on earth did you do to that poor man?"

Irish was instantly defensive. "What am I supposed to have done?"

"That's what I'm asking you. He came home this morning like a—I don't know. Derek said he's never seen him so angry. He was like a thundercloud. Packed up and went straight back to New York. Irish, you spoiled not only his weekend, but ours, too. What happened?"

Irish felt backed into a corner with Doris being a baying dog. "Nothing happened." She sighed and shook her head. "If you must know, I said no."

"You couldn't have. He spent the night, didn't he?"

"I fell asleep. He spent the night on the couch."

Doris smiled. "That must have been jolly exciting for him. Is that what made him mad?"

Another long sigh escaped Irish. "No. He wanted me to go out to dinner tonight and I refused."

"Why on earth would you do that?" Doris's eyes were wide in dismay.

"Because I didn't want to get involved."

"Why not? Is there something wrong with him?"

"No—I mean yes. He's too attractive, too attentive, too—too everything."

Doris laughed. "Now I've heard everything. You send a handsome, eligible man packing because he's too *attractive?*"

"It wouldn't have worked, Doris. I just know it." She felt so defensive.

"Sounds to me like you didn't give him a chance."

"I know. That's what he said." She reached and turned off the fire from under the wine sauce.

"Doris, there are things about me I don't believe you know."

"What? Have you got herpes?"

"No-o." The word reflected her disgust that her friend would even suggest it.

"Then what're you talking about? Your deafness?"

Irish gaped at her. "You know?"

"Of course I know. I have since the first time I met you—well, maybe the second."

"But you never *said* anything."

"Why should I? It's never mattered to me. I was curious, but I figured you'd talk about it when you wanted to. Is that why you sent Geoff away?"

Irish nodded.

"You really are silly."

"You don't know what the problems are between a hearing and nonhearing person."

"I'm sure I don't. But if I had a handsome, prosperous, and very *nice* man after me, I'd sure be willing to take a few chances."

Irish pursed her lips. There was a simple, straightforward logic to Doris's statement which could not be denied. "Okay, so I goofed. Too late now. He's gone back to New York." There was a finality to that statement which deepened her dejection.

Doris Parkins studied her a moment. "I'm sorry. I really didn't come over here to scold you." She put her arm around her. "I must say you look a little hangdog. You did like him, didn't you?"

"A lot. I feel awful, Doris."

"Wanna come over—maybe go out to dinner?"

"No. I have to stay here and work it out."

First thing Monday morning Irish drove up to the deaf school in Hartford, so long an important part of her life, for her regular weekly session with Dr. Arnold Kovacs. He was a good bit more to her than just her speech therapist. Graying, in his mid-fifties, thoroughly avuncular, he was a father figure to her, a source of unstinting affection and encouragement, an admirer, sometimes a confidant, always a person who made her feel good.

She was determined to speak normally, but this was not easy on the basis of the memory of speech last heard when she was twelve. One problem was vocabulary. She maintained a running list of words she had only read, but never heard—new words, technical terms. She used the dictionary for meaning and phonetic pronunciation, but still she needed to go over the words with Dr. Kovacs, getting the precise vowel sounds, accents, and rhythm of the words. He added other words and frequently new slang expressions which had not yet reached the dictionary and were difficult for her to learn.

By far the biggest problem was intonation. Hearing people listen to their own voice and automatically correct their speech to achieve the desired tone of voice and proper emphasis. Irish could do none of that and worried constantly that her voice would become a monotone in which she uttered the proper words but without the lilt, rhythm, tone, and emphasis—the singsong of normal speech. Dr. Kovacs was the only person she trusted to point out her errors and correct her. He talked to her and gave her things to read aloud, stopping her frequently to make refinements in her speech, most of them quite subtle. She felt a bit like Liza Doolittle.

"I'm not doing very well, am I?"

Kovacs rendered a small, noncommittal shrug.

"Not badly, but I've seen my star pupil do much better. You seem a little flat, as though you're lacking your usual enthusiasm. Are you upset about something?"

She nodded. "A little, yes."

"Want to talk about it?"

She looked at the soft brown eyes behind the steel-rimmed glasses, the smiling mouth hidden within his beard. It was salt and pepper now, trimmed short and curly. There was a grizzly look to him which belied his kindly nature. "Oh, it's nothing. I met a man I liked. It—it didn't work out."

"I see, an affair of the heart." He laughed. "Afraid I can't help you there."

"He was a hearing person, doctor."

"That hardly makes him the enemy."

"The problems would be very great. You have to know that."

"True." He pulled down the corners of his mouth as an expression of disagreement. "Many couples have overcome them. When there is love, it is possible—"

"I know it worked for you and Mrs. Kovacs, but—"

"Yes, thirty-five years."

"—I know it wouldn't with Geoff and me. I'm sure of it."

He looked at her a long moment, studying her face. "Very well. If you're convinced, I'm convinced. I just know a woman as talented and attractive as you cannot remain unattached forever—at least I hope not." He changed the subject. "Could I ask you to do me a favor, Irish?"

If there was one person who could ask anything of her it was this man. "Of course."

"We have a young woman here at the school.

Heather Whiting. Been here a couple of years. Similar situation to yours, Irish. She went deaf at fifteen —mumps, I think."

Irish had an instinctive understanding of what he was going to ask, but allowed him to do so. She interrupted only to ask her age.

"Heather is seventeen—very bright and quick. Quite a pretty girl. We've taught her all the tools. Her lipreading and speech are—well, adequate. But she'll lose them quickly if she doesn't use them." He sighed. "That's the problem. She remains depressed, withdrawn. Thinks her life is over, I assume. She needs to discover it is just beginning. There are lots of opportunities for—"

"I know."

"I thought she might relate to someone who has had the same experience. Would you take her under your wing a bit, talk to her, show her—"

"Of course. I'll do it today. She can come home with me. She'll probably love the beach."

He grinned. "I knew I could count on you. I'll arrange it at once."

"Just one thing, doctor. Don't tell her I'm deaf."

He seemed about to protest, then nodded his understanding.

As usual Dr. Kovacs had understated. Heather Whiting was more beautiful than pretty, with long blonde hair and vivid blue eyes. With her slender figure she was a shoo-in to have many boyfriends, except that she was entirely withdrawn, little more than monosyllabic. But as Irish figured, a day at the beach proved too attractive a lure, and the girl came along with her. At the car she actually burst out laughing. Sam sat upright behind the wheel of the little MG, waiting for Irish to return. He did it whenever she left the car, never failing to garner attention.

"He looks like he's the driver."

Irish saw Heather smile and delighted in it. "I suspect he thinks he is." As she scooted Sam over and slid under the wheel, Heather getting in the passenger side, she added, "There's a bonus. I don't have to worry about anyone ripping off the car when I'm not in it." As they drove home in silence Sam made a new girlfriend.

At the cottage it was difficult at first. Heather retreated into her shell, and Irish's attempts to draw her out took on the character of a cross-examination, with the girl offering little more than one-word answers. But Irish did learn that she was from New London where her father was an officer in nuclear subs, away a lot. She had an older brother, also in the Navy, and a younger sister.

"I'll bet you have a boyfriend."

"No."

"Really? I'd think a girl like you would be fighting them off." She saw her shake her head. "Why not?"

Heather looked at her with disapproval. "Don't con me. You know I'm deaf."

"That hardly precludes boyfriends." Her own words shocked her. What about the way she'd treated Geoff—rejecting him without even giving him a chance. Heather's situation was different from hers, she rationalized, knowing in her heart that it wasn't really true. "C'mon," she continued with a smile, "there must be someone you care about."

Heather shrugged. "I used to."

"What was his name?"

"Doug."

"You don't see him anymore?"

"No."

"Why not?" No answer. "Because you're deaf?" No answer.

The tension was relieved when Heather asked, "Are you an artist?"

"No, illustrator." She explained the difference then, showed her some of her work. Heather began to open up, asking questions, taking an interest.

"Are you famous?"

"Hardly, but I do keep busy. My work is in demand. It didn't used to be." She told of her early struggles. "Say, would you like to pose for me? I do a lot of work from photographs—all illustrators do. Models are too expensive."

Heather hesitated. "I—I don't think so."

"Oh, come on. You have an interesting face. I can use you sometime. You'll be immortalized on a book jacket or something."

Irish set up her Polaroid on the tripod and began to photograph Heather, gradually getting her to relax, smile, turn her body as a model, assume various roles. As Heather looked at the pictures later she was radiant. "That was fun."

"You were very good. You photograph beautifully. Nice cheekbones." The smile Irish earned, the brightness in the girl's eyes, made it all worth the effort. "Shall we try the beach as promised?"

They spent a long time running Sam, swimming, frolicking in the water, lying in the sun. Although the need to work nagged at her mind, Irish tried to give herself completely to Heather, fully aware she was enjoying herself. Heather Whiting really was an ebullient person, reacting to praise of her energy and athletic ability. Back in the house, Irish made ham sandwiches for a late lunch. They ate on the porch in their swimsuits, an attentive Sam observing every bite they took.

"Do you like Dr. Kovacs?" Irish asked.

"I guess so."

"Only guess? Then you don't know him. I don't know what I'd do without him."

Heather seemed puzzled. "You know him?"

"Of course. I've been going to him for years—every Monday morning."

The girl's eyes widened in surprise. "You're *deaf?*"

"Didn't you know? What do you think I was doing at the deaf school?"

"I-I—" Heather's mouth was open. She seemed speechless.

"I lost my hearing when I was twelve. I go to Dr. Kovacs to maintain my speech."

Heather seemed unable to recover from her surprise. "I can't believe it. You're so. . . . You don't act deaf."

"How is a deaf person supposed to act?" She smiled. "Really, Heather, being deaf isn't the end of the world. You and I are lucky. We have speech and with effort we can keep it. And we can lip-read. We don't have to wear a sign around our necks declaring our deafness to the world."

"Do people know you're deaf?"

"I don't know. I suspect—I hope—people I meet casually, store clerks, waiters, people like that, have no idea. But I'm far from certain what they know. I simply don't make an issue of it. I hardly go around saying I'm deaf if I don't absolutely have to. People pretty much take you as you are."

"Don't you get asked about it?"

"From strangers? Almost never. Only once or

twice, I think." She smiled. "People don't pay as much attention to us as we think."

"But your friends, do they know?"

Irish hesitated, remembering Doris—and Geoff. "I'd like to think they don't." She sighed. "But I guess that's not really possible. I'm sure they say things behind my back which I don't hear. They must notice I don't react to sounds as they do." She pursed her lips. Saying all this was suddenly difficult. She felt she was revealing herself. But when she looked at the expectant eyes of this girl she knew she had to go on. "I have a good friend, Doris. We see a lot of each other—tennis, shopping, things like that. It was only a couple of days ago that I discovered she knew all along I was deaf. I'd never said anything and she never brought it up, so. . . ." Irish let a shrug finish the sentence. "You see, Heather, being deaf, any handicap for that matter, doesn't matter between real friends. Doris treats me—" she laughed "—just as nastily as she does everyone else. I'm sure she understands I can't talk on the phone. If she wants to talk to me she comes over. Other friends drop me a note inviting me to parties and such. It works out."

"How did you lose your hearing?"

"Spinal meningitis. Look, Heather, I understand how you feel, what you're going through. That's why Dr. Kovacs asked me to talk to you. You feel lost, bewildered, and depressed. The bottom has dropped out of your world. You feel like . . . like a stranger on your own planet. Everything is foreign. You don't know how to act or what to do. So you retreat into yourself, creating your own private world. Isn't that about it?"

Heather nodded. "Yes."

"You can't, Heather. I won't let you. When I went

deaf I was just as lost as you are—maybe more so because I was younger, less able to cope. Then a few months later I lost my family in a plane crash, my mother, my father, my little sister. I was utterly alone, Heather. Oh, I had an uncle and his family on the West Coast, but I hardly knew them. I had no one."

"That's awful! You must've been—"

"Yes. I was devastated. I don't know what would have happened to me if it hadn't been for Dr. Kovacs. He and his wife and children became my family. They made me feel loved, wanted, important. Gradually I found the courage to break out of my shell, go out in the world, confront it and adapt. Drawing and painting had always been my escape. I used it to create a fantasy world of my desires where I was all the things I thought I was not: beautiful, desired, sought-after, loved—and hearing. One day Dr. Kovacs showed some of my work to an art director for an ad agency. He encouraged me, eventually bought a couple of my things. I discovered I could make it as an illustrator. I might not be able to talk on the phone. I might not get into communications and a lot of other things. But I could make a living by drawing. I could be independent, self-support-ing, my own person."

"I can't draw."

"But there are lots of things you can do. You're very athletic. Did you know there was a deaf diver in the last Olympics? He could lip-read in two languages." Irish smiled. "And a deaf girl was a finalist in one of the major beauty contests not long ago. I forget which one. You could try that."

"That's silly."

"Not very. A little makeup here and there and you'd knock 'em dead." She laughed. "But I am being silly. The point is there are lots of things the deaf do super well. After all, we aren't distracted by the phone and all the other stuff that goes on. What are you interested in?''

Heather hesitated. "I'd thought about computer programming."

"There you go. You'll be a whiz—but not if you stay in your shell. You have to break out—go for it."

"I suppose."

"No supposing, Heather. You have to go out in the world, meet people, be with them. So you'll be hurt once in awhile. So you'll feel foolish from time to time. But you'll find most people are pretty good if you give them a chance." Her own hypocrisy stunned her. *You won't even give me a chance.* Geoff, oh Geoff!

"What's the matter?"

Irish swallowed, rendered a wan smile. "Nothing. I was distracted. What was I saying? Oh yes, give people a chance. Have you kept in touch with your friends?"

"No."

"You should. I'll bet they miss you."

Heather shook her head. "I don't think so."

"But you don't know. Try it. Look them up, drop in. Doug, for example. I'll bet he's pining away for you. Do you know where he is?"

"He's in college, up at Storrs, UConn."

"Drop him a note, Heather. What have you got to lose but your shell?"

Irish drove her back to Hartford that afternoon, a far more confident and outgoing person than when she left. Her good-bye was a prolonged hug and a profusion of "thank yous" and promises to follow her advice.

Irish had a good feeling about the day, but it

faded as she drove back to Westport with Sam. Depression weighed on her until it was painful. She could think only of Geoff and how she had sent him away, certain now she had been wrong, hopelessly wrong. He had deserved a chance and she hadn't given it. "You're fantastic, Irish. What gall you have giving advice to others? Physician, heal thyself."

Back at the cottage she considered writing to Geoff to say she was sorry. But what was the use? She had hurt him. He had fled to New York and who could blame him? Let it be. Probably for the best anyway. But wasn't it amazing how much he had gotten under her skin—and in so short a time? But there was a cure, wasn't there—the one really important thing in her life. She went directly to her drawing board and started to work.

FIVE

By Friday Irish was halfway pleased with herself. The book jacket was almost finished—and the hero emerging in acrylic on her easel did not look like Geoff Winter. She had used a photograph of Mrs. Harrington's son next door.

Despite working from early morning till late at night, she had not entirely succeeded in exorcising Geoff Winter from her mind. He was still there, simmering on the back burner, ready to boil over when she stopped work. The nights were especially bad, his touch, his remembered kisses preying on her mind. Worse was the knowledge she had no one to blame but herself for having lost him. She had sent him away and for no good reason. But she was doing pretty well. Probably ought to thank him for all the work she was getting done—if she ever saw him again. So she wasn't exactly happy. So she had this nagging feeling that something was missing from her life. Lots of people did. The human condition, no doubt.

It was just before dark when he came, announced by an exuberant Sam. As she let him in she felt, first, a profound sense of relief, then a strange stricture in her throat.

He wore a linen sports jacket, tan in color, brown slacks, white shirt, and tie. Apparently he had come straight from his office. He seemed tense, nervous, the gaze he fixed on her was guarded and penetrating, as though he were searching for telltale signs of her reaction to him. "I worked out a tax plan for you. Thought I'd bring it out, discuss it with you. Hope you don't mind."

Tears filled her blue eyes. "Thank God for the IRS," she said, or hoped she did. The lump in her throat made it difficult to speak.

Sam intruded, jumping on Geoff, wanting to be greeted. With what seemed to be great reluctance, Geoff turned to the dog, petting him vigorously. He returned to her. "What did you say? I couldn't hear for Sam."

"I said—" She managed a swallow. "I said I'm glad to see you."

"Me too."

What was in his eyes? Longing, desire, and yes, an appeal.

"You're even lovelier than I remembered."

She looked down at her splattered smock, then back at him, shaking her head, struggling against the sob building in her throat. She wiped away a tear with her fingertips.

"It's been a hellish week, Irish."

She nodded. "Yes, awful."

Her body seemed to have a mind of its own. All it wanted was to be pressed against Geoff, encircled within his arms. But she resisted and that seemed strange to her. Turning away, she went to her easel, removed her smock. She wore a blue tank top underneath.

"Is that your book jacket?"

"Yes."

"You did all that this week? It's almost finished."

She nodded, then tried to smile. "I have you to thank."

"Me?"

"I felt so lousy about sending you away. All I could do was . . . was work. It kept me from thinking about—"

"I know. Same with me. About all I did was work on your taxes. Mistake, I guess. I kept having such a sense of you." He smiled. "Amazing what you can learn about a person by studying their tax records."

"What did you learn?"

"That I can't stay away from you, Irish."

He came to her then. She was certain he was going to take her in his arms and she wanted him to. But he hesitated. She knew he wanted to but was somehow constrained. He turned to her painting. "That's very good. The man looks really surprised."

"I had a lot of trouble with it." She smiled. "The first couple of days every face I drew looked like yours. Finally I used the boy next door as a model."

"I'm jealous."

"Only his photograph."

"Oh, Irish." His strong hands came to her shoulders and began massaging them. "All I could think of all week was you. I had to see you."

She was so filled with emotion she could only nod.

"I know there'll be problems. I can see situations that might come up. Some will be bummers. But can't we work them out—somehow? All I know is I have to try."

She nodded repeatedly, fighting back her tears, trying to swallow.

"I'm miserable, Irish. I can't just walk away and forget you. Seeing you again I know that more than ever. All I ask is a chance. We can work it out. I know we can."

"Yes, yes," she managed to utter.

"It's a cinch we can't go on this way. Life is too—"

"I know."

Suddenly he stopped his stream of words and smiled. It was a grin really, quite boyish, revealing his delight. "Do you mean that?"

"Yes. I want to see you, Geoff. I need to."

His thumbs stroked both her cheeks, slowly, a maddening whisper of a caress, and his eyes seemed to penetrate deep within her. Then she was in his arms, pressed hard against him, her cheek against his. The shameless tears were welling out of her now. Then his hand was in her hair and she looked into his eyes, which were filled with tenderness and longing, just before his lips descended on hers. With his mouth he claimed her, telling her how much he desired her and how completely he would satisfy her. She was unable to stop trembling from the hot urgent sensations this man aroused in her. She felt his warm breath on her ear. His lips moved but she didn't know what he was saying. She pushed away from him a little to see his mouth. "Please tell me what you said."

He shook his head. "I'm sorry. All week I've reminded myself that I can't whisper in your ear." He smiled. "Somehow you make me forget everything. I asked if you're sure, really sure. I don't want to—"

"You're not." She blinked, swallowed. "I want you, too. I want the chance—our chance. If it doesn't work out—"

"I'll see that it does."

"What's the old saying? Better to have loved and lost."

"We won't lose, Irish."

She closed her eyes tightly and thought, *I wish I could believe you.*

He kissed her again, but the joining of mouths, each eager to discover the other, did not last nearly long enough. An impatient Sam jumped up on both of them. Geoff tried to pet him while clinging to her, then gave up in laughter. "We've a problem already. This guy's a crowd."

Irish watched him bend to Sam, rub his head and ears. He was saying something to the dog which she couldn't hear. She felt so strange, as though her insides were quivering with anticipation. She understood. Having committed herself to him, she only wanted its fulfillment. He looked up at her and asked if she'd eaten. She shook her head.

"Do you want to go out to dinner?"

The question was an intrusion, the mundane, forcing reality upon them. "I don't know. I-I guess so."

He kissed her then, so gently, so softly, the tender surfaces of their lips brushing against each other. The effect was timorous, a prelude of pleasures to come. At its end she looked at him, saw the burning desire in his eyes, which reflected her own, and then glanced away. Everything seemed so strange. "D-do you want a drink or—or something?"

He smiled. "I had such great plans. I was going to take you out to dinner, be a gentleman, be patient, not rush you, let nature take its course."

"I think it already has."

He led her to the bedroom—or did she lead him? —closing the door on a mystified Sam. The darkness added intimacy to their embrace and she felt the heat of him, smelled his masculinity. He seemed so right, their mouths so perfect in their fit, his body made for hers, and when his tongue came to her she accepted it as the fount of the sensations which

71

swirled through her. For a long time she was unable to let go of him.

Still holding Geoff's hand, she made her way on unsteady legs to the bed and turned on the light beside it. There were long shadows she had never noticed before, hers falling on him.

"The light isn't necessary, Irish."

"I want to see you—share with you."

She slid his jacket from him, dropping it on the chair, then fumbled with his tie, unbuttoned his shirt, finally thrusting her arms around his waist. The contact was electric, making her bare arms tingle. Beneath her hands, his skin was smooth yet underlaid with muscle. She felt rather than heard his quickened breath and knew from his rough, insistent kiss that he was becoming aroused.

With gentle pressure she made him sit on the edge of the bed and gently kissed him, then started to pull off her tank top. He stopped her, wanting to do it himself. She raised her arms and it was gone, then his arms came around her, unfastening her bra. She watched his eyes as he pulled the undergarment away, and was rewarded by the expression on his face—a combination of delight, wonder, and a hint of gratitude.

"You're so lovely," he murmured.

There was nothing for her to say.

His gaze rose to her eyes, then lowered again to her pink-tipped breasts. "What are you thinking?"

"That my cup runneth over."

"I feel I'm receiving a gift, a precious one. And I am—you."

His touch made her gasp, so sensitized was she. Starting at her waist, his fingers rose slowly as though savoring each inch of her, reluctant to move

72

on, finally reaching her breasts, cupping them with gentle pressure.

"You're so soft."

Her breasts felt swollen, filled with a sweet ache, and the risen tips seemed drawn to his revolving thumb, caressing fingers. Sensations buffeted her, striking deep, making her tremble with desire, and she had to close her eyes and lean against her hands resting on his shoulders. Her world became one governed utterly by sensations, which grew ever stronger and more pleasurable as he intensified his movements, caressing her back, gently kneading her breasts, sliding his hand over her thigh.

"Oh, Geoff, that feels so good. . . ."

Words were lost as he pulled her closer. She felt sparks shooting down her legs, filling her body as his tongue moved over her, as he took tender tiny bites. He ceased abruptly, only to begin again, intensifying her pleasure. She held his head, her fingers in his hair, guiding him, wanting somehow to have all of herself within him.

"It feels so right—" she shuddered "—like you belong."

He came away then and she opened her eyes to see him say, "I do."

Soon they lay in bed, completely naked now, on their sides, facing each other. Their hands slid up and down each other's body ceaselessly, caressing and searching, their skin so highly sensitized, they quivered with anticipation.

"Oh, Geoff. It's like—like I come alive . . . at your touch."

"Yes. I've never—"

"It's as though our bodies have found each other. . . ."

"Waited their whole lives."

He kissed her then, deeply, his tongue entering, teasing hers, filling her yet only making her ravenous for more. She shuddered and her eyes flickered and closed. She felt like jetsam, floating on a warm sea of exquisite sensation, directed by tides of desire anchored only by Geoff's touch.

She tried to fight the impulse to open her eyes, but she wanted to see him, be with him. He relinquished her mouth. "Close your eyes. Relax and enjoy. You are not alone."

She tried to look at him, swallowing once, gasping for breath, but he lowered his head again, pleasuring her with his mouth and his hands, which skillfully stroked her most intimate places. Her eyelids fluttered, then closed, and in her silent world there were no distractions, no ticking clock, no voices, no sounds from afar, not a rustle or squeak or moan, just his touch flooding over her, creating sweet aches and great need.

There was a pause when he moved on top of her, then the touch of his exploring fingers, another pause as she became his guide, then she was shuddering, gasping, filled at last, feeling complete and whole. Through hooded eyes she saw him above her on extended arms, knew the desire and immeasurable depth of his eyes, then raised her head to look down at their wondrous joining, saw him move but could look no more as she gasped and some sound, unknown to her, escaped her. He moved, again, again and again. A stillness came over her, more pure than any she had ever known. All sensation, all awareness seemed to focus in a single place, known only to her, reachable only by him just before her whole body seemed to dissolve into a paroxysm of shuddering. It went on the longest time, her private rapture.

When at last she could open her eyes, he was smiling down at her. She remained disoriented, still clinging to the echoes of rapture, barely able to swallow, but the movement of his lips reached her consciousness. "I love you, Irish. I always will."

She saw him move, felt him within her, still filling, knew his urgency, then wrapped her legs around his hips to ride with him on whatever journey he took, faster, longer, so different now, with more giving and sharing. Yes, yes, you, too. She felt the power of him, omnipotent, so strong, a greater filling, then came need, so strong, so swift, racing with him, headlong, catching up, thrusting for the finish, bursting over, around, through, with him, shatteringly, truly devastating her.

He lay on his back. She was pressed against him on her side, her head resting on his shoulder, her leg draped over his. He gently caressed her back and side. His touch was soothing, like a balm. She felt satiated, at peace, utterly languid with contentment.

"Do you know one of the really nice things about making love?"

She knew he had spoken but hadn't been watching. She raised her head, looked at his lips, asked him to repeat. She smiled. "I know several things—now. What do you have in mind?"

"This. Did you know that when a woman is satisfied, has truly enjoyed it, she always moves toward the man afterward?"

"Really?"

"So I understand."

She kissed him lightly. "Must be true then."

"Did you hear me say I love you?"

"Yes, I know you said it."

"But you don't believe it—on the theory that

what a man says before or while he's making love is not to be trusted."

"Never thought of it."

"But when a man says it afterward, now that is to be believed. I love you, Irish."

The words thrilled her—but also disturbed her. It was too soon for her. "Geoff—" She pursed her lips, pondering her words. "I can't say it just yet. Can you understand? When I do I want to mean it—forever and ever."

"I mean it."

"I know you do. I'm a lucky girl." The kiss she gave him now was deep and leisurely. When she finished she rested her head on his shoulder. They were quiet for a time, and she enjoyed the languorous stroking of her back, the play of her hand over his chest. Finally he moved so she was on her back, he on his side above her.

"Did I tell you you're something else, Irish lady?"

She smiled up at him. "I don't believe you mentioned it."

"Well, you are. It means a lot to a man to have a woman turn on like that."

Another smile. "It wasn't difficult—with you."

"Did you feel alone, isolated? It wasn't a solitary experience for me. Was it for you?"

"Hmm." She tried to remember. "I suppose—I don't know. When I close my eyes I lose two senses. All I know is your touch. Everything is tactile. It's—it's overwhelming, almost more than I can bear."

"Wow!" He smiled. "No wonder you turn on so completely. It must be like a straight shot, sort of a mainlining sensation."

"I suppose. Maybe it's one of the rewards of deafness." And she smiled. "But to answer your question, no, I guess I wasn't alone. You were there, with me, creating everything." She shivered from the memory.

"You're never going to be alone ever again, Irish."

She watched him slowly descend to kiss her, enjoying his eyes until they distorted in her vision and she had to close hers, leaving only the soft tenderness of his lips. At its end she stroked his cheek, feeling the slight roughness of his whiskers now, running her fingertips around the edge of his lips. "I want to ask you something. What does your voice sound like?"

He smiled. "I have a very high, squeaky voice."

"You don't."

"To me it sounds very deep, resonant, but when I hear it recorded, it's nothing special, just a voice. But you. Now that's special."

"Really?"

"Indeed. It's low."

"Low in tone or sound?"

"Both. Low-pitched, throaty, with an excess of air. I have to pay attention to hear you. It's very sexy."

"Wow!" She grinned. "All that. You're not kidding."

"It's a real turn on. Course everything about you is."

She laughed.

"And you have a nice laugh—sorta wicked."

Happiness seemed to well within her as a spring. "I think maybe I could come to love you."

"I'm working at making you."

She moved to kiss him, then stopped. "Do I sound funny when I talk?"

He shook his head. "No. You sound like people."

"Are you sure? I worry about my voice being too flat, too phony, too anything, too everything."

"I never thought. You can't hear yourself, can you? Is that a problem?"

"Yes. I go to therapy for it. Will you tell me if my voice isn't right, if I get lazy or—"

"It's fine, honey. You're fine—beautiful, gorgeous, lovely." He kissed her. "The only problem you have is keeping me away from you."

"That's no problem."

A real kiss came to her now, deeper, longer, stirring her desire. He looked at her quizzically. "You have three choices: a drink, food, or me."

"Let's take 'em in order."

She donned her terry cloth robe, he his pants, no shirt, and in bare feet padded out to be effusively greeted by a relieved Sam. In the kitchen she set out the whiskey, ice, and glasses for him, then perused the freezer compartment of the refrigerator. "I usually cook, but I keep some TV dinners for emergencies. That all right?"

"Sure."

Suddenly she stared at him. There was a sinking feeling in her stomach.

"What's the matter?"

A moment longer she stared. "Do you realize I've just made love to a man—and I don't even know what he likes to eat?"

He grinned. "Happens all the time."

"Not to me it doesn't. I told you, I don't like one-night stands."

His smile faded quickly and he studied her. "You're serious, aren't you? You're upset." He came to her at the open refrigerator, put his arm around her shoulders. "It wasn't a one-night stand, Irish. I wish I'd known you all my life, that we'd

78

grown up together, but that didn't happen. I'm just glad I found you now—before there is anyone else." He squeezed her tighter. "Look, we'll learn all about each other. You'll find out what kind of toothpaste I use, which leg I put into my pants first, which—"

"Your left."

"It's sort of fun, isn't it? Discovering all the incidental things about each other."

"Yes." She smiled.

He turned to examine the freezer with her. "I'm about to share a secret which I would never dare reveal to my Manhattan friends. I'm from the Midwest. I really am a meat and potatoes man, and if I never have French cooking again I'll be thrilled. Gourmets are near the bottom of my list, but I never dare let on."

She laughed. "I like that—I think." She spotted a carton. "How about Swiss steak, mashed potatoes, and gravy with peas?"

"Heavenly."

He returned to making his drink while she lit the oven, opened the food packages, and began to think about making a salad. Did he want one? She turned to ask, saw his lips moving. He had been talking to her. She hadn't known or heard. The sinking feeling returned to her stomach.

In a moment he noticed, stopped talking. "I'm sorry."

She pursed her lips. "It's all right."

"No, it's not. Look, Irish, I'll learn. I'll remember. It's just that I don't think of you as deaf. Isn't that a little bit good?"

She smiled. "Yes, nice. What were you talking about?"

"I was prattling on, like a dummy, about growing up in Ohio."

"I want to know it all. Just let me make the salad first." He stood beside her, arm around her, snitching bites out of the bowl as she made it. She slapped at his hand once or twice. It was to her tender, wholesome, so much fun, and she realized just how lonely she had been. Inserting the last bit of carrot into his mouth, she asked, "And what kind of dressing does a nongourmet like?"

"Your choice. I must learn to make sacrifices."

"Which means you don't like salads."

"Salads are to be tolerated like slow elevators, busy signals, and—"

"Gourmet cooks."

Over the dinner on the two stools and under her questioning, he told her about himself. He grew up in a small town in Ohio, Gamble's Mill, considerably the youngest—an afterthought, really—of five children. "A good Catholic family," he said, Polish. His real name was Winterowsky. His parents, both gone now, were good people. He loved them. Father was a steelworker, taught thrift, hard work, basic values. His two brothers and two sisters, all married with families, two with grandkids, all lived in the area, factory worker, one an accountant, the other owner of a drycleaning shop. Fine people, a rock for his life, very loving, although they disapproved of his name change and kidded him about his big city "airs."

"You weren't about to be satisfied with that life?"

"No, I wanted out. I knew there was more. I was good at the books—only fair as a jock. I won a scholarship to Williams. That, working, a big loan got me through. Then came Harvard Law. Here I am."

She smiled. "Thank you for telling me. It explains a lot."

"Like what?"

"Oh, I'd spotted a bit of a rough edge to you, as though you weren't quite a finished product. Now I know where it comes from."

"You can take the boy out of the small town, but not the small town out of the boy."

"It's a nice quality, Geoff, very appealing." She shook her head at him. "What about you isn't?"

"Nothing, I hope. Now you. Tell me about your family."

She did, and once again it was a strange mixture of pain and pleasure for her. "My father was in politics—not the running for office kind, but behind the scenes. He worked for the Democratic Party here in Connecticut. I'm not really sure what he did, fund raising, voter registration, administration, seeing the bills were paid, that sort of thing, I guess. He was born in this country, but he was Irish to the core, very well met, happy, upbeat. Everyone loved him. I—I know I did."

She told of her mother, Colleen, real Irish, from Limerick. Came over as a waitress, met her father. So beautiful, Irish temper, couldn't quite get used to American ways, having money. She worried a lot. A good counterweight to her father. "She only ever went on one trip with Dad—the last. It was a private plane. He was taking Mom and my sister Kathleen along to Hot Springs, Arkansas—some party convention. They never arrived."

"You miss them."

"Of course." She sighed. "Oh, I suppose I've romanticized them in my mind. They couldn't have been as marvelous as I remember."

"It's a good way to feel, Irish. Must've been hard for you."

"Yes. I was just beginning to cope with my deafness." Her eyes filled with tears. "I miss Dad particularly. He made me feel important, very loved. He wouldn't let me get down. When he died, all of them died, it sort of knocked the slats out of me."

"No one. Loneliness. Complete isolation."

"That's about it." She sighed. "But I got over it—with help." She told him about Dr. Kovacs, drawing, painting, the start of her career, discovering she could make her own way, find independence.

"Still there is loneliness."

"I—I didn't used to . . . think so." She sniffled, swallowed, wiped away a tear which had spilled over, then found a smile. "That dumb salad did it."

"What d'you mean?"

"Sam can't help me make one." She sighed. "Oh, Geoff, it's so nice having you here. I didn't know I was so lonely."

He put his arm around her, took both her hands in his. "You won't be again, if only. . . ."

She waited for him to go on. "If only what?"

"If only you can find a place for me in your life."

"Oh, Geoff, I want to. I want to so much."

He kissed her then, gently, nibbling at her mouth, pulling her lower lip between his, laving it with the tip of his tongue, sending a gust of sensations through her. She felt her breath shorten and her body trembling. She leaned her mouth hard against his, biting at the source of her pleasure.

"Is there some law against making love on a full stomach?"

He touched her lips with his fingertips. "There shouldn't be if there is."

It was not at all as before. Gone was the urgency,

the overpowering need, the sense of discovery, replaced now by certain knowledge, greater intimacy now, and heightened boldness. Together they probed the frontiers of pleasure and vied to see who could give a greater gift to the other. And when at last the precious stillness came over her, she sensed she was being welded to him mind and body, irrevocably changed. Geoff, blessed Geoff.

She awoke slowly, sleep tugging at her repeatedly. Even when consciousness came, it was filled with memories, so real, of a night of love, his arms encircling her, his body acting as a cradle for hers. She reached out. He was gone. She felt deprived, then remembered. Just at dawn. He had awakened her from deep sleep. The fiery sensations had come from so far away, so quietly, stirring her, overriding her, ultimately shattering her. It was as though her mind never fully awakened and only her body had responded. Did it ever!

She threw back the sheet, arose, put on her robe, ran a brush through her hair. She felt languid, so relaxed, dreamy, anything but ready to begin the day. He was sitting on the couch, hunched over the coffee table, pencil in hand. A coffee cup was beside him.

He looked up, smiled. "Good morning, sleepyhead."

She glanced at her mother's clock. Quarter to ten. "At least it's still morning." She smiled. "Do you infect everyone with narcolepsy?"

He laughed. "Sometimes. I found the makings for coffee. Want some?"

"I think I better."

He brought it to her and she cradled it in both hands, sipping. "What are you working on?"

"Your taxes. I want to finish up, explain it to you. We'll do it later."

She noticed he was dressed differently, blue polo shirt, jeans, running shoes. "Where'd you get the clothes?"

"From the car."

She saw his leather grip on the couch and made a face. "So you knew all along this was going to happen. You're rotten."

He grinned. "Only hoped. I figured I'd probably spend the night at Derek's."

She smiled. "I'm glad you didn't." She set down her coffee cup, and placed both her arms around his neck. "The things you do to me."

"I was inspired." He kissed her gently, as if he were sealing what had transpired between them. "I knew you'd be like this—so lovely, soft, languorous, very inviting."

He bent toward her again but she moved away, laughing. "There must be another activity we can enjoy. Have you had breakfast?"

"I waited for you."

"Let me shower first."

There began for her—for them—an idyllic weekend filled with play, laughter, fun, and love, all suffused with a sense of discovery. They ran Sam's legs off—and hers, frolicked in the water, laid in the burning sun holding hands—at least until neither could stand it anymore and retreated to the cottage to make love, rapturous love, sweaty, superheated bodies slipping and sliding to fulfillment. He was a tease, she discovered, and had a capacity to be just plain silly. She couldn't remember ever laughing so much. He was tireless, full of energy, a dominating physical presence, and she had a sense of being small, vulnerable, capable of being overpowered by him, yet also protected, safe. It was a new feeling for her, very attractive. And he was wholly attentive to her, sharing himself, leaving no doubt he wanted to be with her, and that was attractive, too.

There were problems. The cottage was small, cluttered with her life. He seemed too big for it and lacked space for himself. Something would have to be done about that. He forgot her deafness a few times, calling to her from the bathroom or kitchen, speaking behind her back. But each time he corrected himself, laughed, teased her about what he'd really said, sometimes making up utter foolishness.

They talked a lot, about nothing and everything, life in Westport, what she did with her time, friends, her work, being deaf, his work, his life in Manhattan, the joys and oppressions of single life. There was inquisitiveness to him which she liked, and candor, openness to ideas and opinions. She concluded Geoff Winter was an honest man. What you saw was what you got.

They went out to dinner Saturday night. Irish dressed to the nines in a blue chiffon, a bit frilly for her usual tastes, very slimming. She had bought it some time before because it was so beautiful, but had never worn it, in part because she never went to the right affair but mostly because it was too daring, bare arms and shoulders, just tiny straps, too much cleavage. Geoff liked it. She saw it in his eyes.

They drove to a rustic but elegant inn near Darien. She felt beautiful and, strangely, not uncomfortable under the stares she knew she was gaining.

"You do realize everyone's looking at you, don't you?"

"Hardly. It's you. They've never seen such a handsome man."

"Sure. And the sun rises in the west, too."

She felt comfortable with him. He had that hard-to-describe quality every woman looks for in a man, ease, familiarity, confidence as he went about the business of obtaining a table and being seated. She felt he was taking charge of her. And he conveyed a subtle intimacy. He was with *her*, no one else.

The waiter came for their drink order. She hesitated, trying to decide whether to have her usual white wine or brave a cocktail.

"He wants to know what you want to drink."

She blinked, startled. She knew what the waiter wanted. She looked up at him. "A vodka gimlet please, straight up, very dry." Geoff ordered a Scotch on the rocks. Why had he repeated what the waiter said?

"You surprise me." He smiled, the one that proved his delight in her. "I didn't know you were into martinis."

"I didn't either." She smiled, a letting go of her pique. It hadn't meant anything. "I seem to be surprising myself quite a lot of late."

"But you like the result?"

She shook her head and looked at him through squinted eyes. "I hate it, can't you tell?"

He was holding her hand across the table when their drinks came. They raised their glasses and he toasted her, her loveliness, their happiness, their future.

"As I said, my cup runneth over." She sipped, swallowed. It tasted vile, but she wouldn't let on. Again his hand returned to hers and again she felt that electric sensation only he seemed to produce. She had a sense of him as all eyes—for her.

"Remember the song, people will say we're in love?"

She knew he was singing something, but had no way to know the melody. "I don't think so."

His smile faded abruptly. "Goofed again, didn't I? You can't hear music."

That didn't help. "Isn't it an old song? I think I remember it."

"Yes, *Oklahoma*, Rodgers and Hammerstein."

She saw his distress. "It's all right, Geoff. These things are bound to happen." She smiled, a reassurance. "I'm not glass. I won't break. Do you like music?"

He did and that led to a discussion of some Broadway shows he'd seen.

"I'd like to go sometime."

He seem surprised. "But—"

"I know, but I'd still like to be there, be part of it all."

"Consider it done."

She saw the admiration in his eyes. "Did you know I can dance? I'm quite light on my feet—and proud of it."

"You can't!"

"Live music, not recorded. I feel the music—" She smiled. "At least I hope I do. There's something about the way they hold their instruments— or maybe it's vibrations." She laughed. "Or maybe I'm just making a fool of myself."

"You're amazing."

The problem came when they ordered dinner. Again Geoff kept repeating what the waiter asked— how the filet was to be cooked, what vegetable, what salad dressing. She was annoyed, then embarrassed. She sensed the waiter knew there was something wrong with her. It angered her, threatening to destroy the whole evening.

Always empathetic, Geoff touched her hand,

made her look at him, asked what was wrong. She wished he hadn't. She didn't want to look at him—not just now. She had to find a way to cope with her disappointment.

Again he compelled her attention. "Don't shut me out, Irish. This isn't going to work if we aren't totally honest with each other."

She looked at him a long moment. Yes, he was right. She had to speak. "Geoff, I've been ordering meals in restaurants long before I met you. I know what the waiter said. I know what I want to eat. You're not the only person I understand. By repeating everything he said you made me feel like a—a freak. The waiter now thinks there's something wrong with me."

She saw him bristle. "You asked me to help you."

"That's not the kind of help I need, Geoff. If he'd had an accent, mumbled or something so I couldn't understand, then I might have asked you what he said. But this way—" She stopped, her irritation dissipated by its very expression. But she watched him carefully. He struggled with his own anger, then let it go with a long exhale of air.

"You're right. I'm a sap."

She smiled at him, reached for his hand across the table. "But a dear one."

The rest of the evening went fine. Indeed, the incident seemed to draw them closer. It was as though it helped them make a commitment to candor, to having a direct, simple, very honest relationship. They discussed what it would mean, why it was so necessary for her.

"I remember your saying you have to take words very literally."

"Not all the time, not when I know the person."

She smiled. "You've kidded me all day. I've loved it. I don't want you to stop."

"Then what do you mean by literal?"

She hesitated, seeking words. "Geoff, I don't know if it's possible between two people. All we can do is try." Again she hesitated. "Darling, I don't want you, me, either of us to ever say anything we don't mean, really mean. Let's not pretend, cover up. If you're angry, say so. If you're bored, annoyed, don't like something, want to do something else, then just say so. Let's not have to guess what the other really wants or feels. That's hard for me."

"I understand. Trouble is I don't always know what I want or feel. I don't think anyone does."

"I know that."

"We all go along hoping it'll work out. Usually it does."

"But when it doesn't I want to know."

"Honey, we all have to do things we don't want to. It's life."

"Our life?"

He nodded. "I know what you're saying. I won't con you, Irish. That's a promise."

All she could do was look at him in admiration, respect, and love, for the table bearing coffee cups, brandy, the dregs of dinner separated them. Squeezing his fingers was a poor substitute for what she really wanted to do.

He sensed it. "Shall we go?"

"Not yet. I have something to say. Dumb me. I made such a production out of it, when there were a dozen times I felt it and should have said it naturally. Geoff Winter, I love you." She saw his eyes, knew the brightness of her own. "Nice words, aren't they?"

"And I love you." He grinned. "And I always say what I mean."

On Sunday morning they rose early. Irish worked on her book jacket while Geoff pored over her taxes, then he left her alone while he took Sam for a long walk. That Sunday morning may have been the best of times for her. She felt an inner contentment in having him there, knowing he was working beside her. She was surprised at how much she could concentrate, how well her work went.

That afternoon he said, "I've been thinking about taking a few days off. Things are slow at the office. I've a brief to work on—a court case coming up after Labor Day—but I could work on it here. What d'you think?"

She pursed her lips. "An appealing idea."

"But only an idea."

"No." She smiled now. "I love having you here. I want to be with you."

"Are you sure?"

She shook her head. "No, I'm not sure at all. I guess I'm not very good at living for today and not worrying about the future." She looked at him a long moment very seriously. "But it's not too late to learn. Yes, let's spend as much time together as we can, see what happens."

He came to her, his hands at her waist, kissed her gently. "I'll never hurt you, Irish."

"Yes, you will. We always hurt the one we love. It's part of the price for loving, isn't it?"

SIX

Monday morning she drove with Sam up to Hartford while Geoff returned to the city to take care of business and pick up a few things from his apartment.

Her session with Dr. Kovacs went well, although she avoided too many explanations for her ebullience. She was more confiding in Heather, whom she took to lunch. "I followed my own advice. I'd met a man, a very nice man, but I sent him away. I was afraid of the consequences, being hurt."

"He came back?"

"Yes—thankfully."

"You look very happy."

"I am."

She told her about Geoff, although hardly anything intimate, answering many questions about what he looked like, where he worked, lived. Then she happily learned Heather had written to Doug, earned an immediate reply, and had a date for next weekend.

On the drive back to Westport she thought more seriously about Geoff and what she was doing. He had already invaded her life, irrevocably changing her in ways she was sure she hardly knew. One was obvious, the physical. The word *ecstasy* kept coming to her. She had read it often in books, thinking it sort of corny and overblown, but now, with her new knowledge, she decided it wasn't that bad a word.

The things he had done, they had done! Would this feeling ever go away, the sense of specialness, yes, breathless anticipation? Silly. She was acting like a schoolgirl. But wasn't it nice?

He was coming tonight, staying. A few days, he'd said. In a few days, if they continued as the weekend, she'd be so committed to him there'd be no way ever to get him out from under her skin. To her dog, riding beside her, the top down enjoying the wind in his face, she said, "It's already too late to worry about that, isn't it, Sam? All we can do is go on and hope for the best—no, believe in the best." In Westport, as an act of commitment, she stopped at her doctor's office, got a prescription for The Pill, and had it filled.

At the cottage she busied herself making room for him. It was a hardship, for the place was crammed and cluttered already, but she declared it a labor of love, making space in the closet, emptying a drawer in the dresser, finding room in the medicine chest. She took down her stockings and hung a fresh towel for him. When she finished she had a significant pile of clothes she seldom or never wore. What to do with them? She knew. She took them downtown to the Goodwill store, then raced back. He was waiting in front of the house when she arrived. The first thing she did after she kissed him was to give him a house key.

Thus it truly began for Irish, a time of discovery and the full flowering of love. She felt immersed in masculinity, the scents of shaving cream and cologne, the novel clutter of razor and male appurtenances, a new brand of toothpaste, belts, shoes, dropped socks and apparel draped over chair backs, his books, his papers, heavens, just his presence. He filled doorways, rooms, the whole cottage, charging the familiar with expectancy. Her habits changed, what and when she ate, her attire, where she went, the entire routine of her day. And she did not lament the loss of her rut. This was wonderful. He was wonderful.

Vistas opened up to her. She had television, but seldom watched it, even the closed caption programming. She could lip-read those that weren't, but it took effort and she missed too much when actors spoke off camera or turned away to utter their lines. Geoff made it more enjoyable, telling her what she missed so she could follow the plot better. And he was not bothered when she simply ignored the set and read.

"There are advantages to being deaf, aren't there? You don't hear all the stupid commercials."

"I suppose there are lots of things a person would just as soon not hear."

"Better believe it. The telephone, for instance. It really is more nuisance than convenience. I suspect the United States would have the greatest economic boom in history if we jerked out the phone system. Just think of all the high priced executive time wasted on the phone. Three quarters of every phone call is small talk, hemming and hawing, various foolishness. The thing is a constant distraction. If I want to get anything done at the office I have to refuse all calls—and that seldom works. There are always calls I just *have* to take. If you think about it, this country built its industrial might without the telephone. Everything was done by mail, telegraph, messenger. Worked fine, probably better. Did you know General Douglas MacArthur fought World War II without a phone in his office?"

"He didn't!"

"That's probably why we won—in the Pacific at least."

"It would be nice to have a phone for emergencies, to chat with people."

"True. Maybe we should look upon the phone as a purely social instrument, no business use at all." He laughed. "That'll be the day."

She loved it. He was full of ideas and opinions, often outrageous ones, and she felt he was opening up her mind, blowing out the cobwebs of convention. It was a revelation just how much she'd missed another human being to talk to at home.

He worked part of each day and with a high level of concentration, pouring through law books, making notes on yellow legal pads, then dictating into a tape recorder, pacing constantly as he did so, stopping only to delve into his books again. At such times he all but ignored her and that was fine, for she began the painting of England's Elizabeth I and made great progress. It was enough, more than enough to have him there.

She glanced at him sometimes, reading his lips a little as he dictated, but not really following the subject matter. She liked what she saw. He exuded confidence, authority, command, even. He seemed kinetic with energy, and she suspected he might be difficult to work for, hard-charging, demanding, impatient. She asked him if that was so. He admitted it, saying, "I fear I don't suffer fools gladly." Privately she suspected he could be an intimidating force when he wanted or needed to be, certain that if she was on the jury, she'd vote with him every time.

She discovered he had a switch in his brain. Work done, he flicked it to play. Physical activity was an important outlet for him, especially in the late afternoon. He played with the same energy he used in work, and she understood how he stayed in shape. Sam found all he could bargain for in him, then came strenuous tennis, a hard swim—all done as fun, not a chore. Irish knew she couldn't compete with him, but she did her best. He usually posed a wager on tennis or a foot or swimming race, and she invariably lost—only to win when the wager was collected in the bedroom.

That part of their relationship remained at white heat, which surprised her. She expected familiarity to dampen their fires. It didn't happen. Sometimes a touch, even a glance would ignite them. And at the oddest times—in the middle of the word *of*, as he put it. He always seemed to find a way to arouse her. Best, she felt certain knowledge she was beautiful, desired, and loved, wanted, needed. She felt suffused with sensuality, somehow glowing with promise—fulfilled promise.

"You're turning me into a wanton," she complained teasingly.

"As long as you want only me."

He was more impulsive, outgoing, and social than her, a product, she decided, of his energy and inquisitiveness. He liked to drive around, looking at houses, finding old buildings, monuments, or just a scenic spot, a graveyard, an isolated stretch of beach. He browsed through stores, picking up an item or two, knicknacks or a book, discovering what she liked and buying it for her. They ate out most evenings, and he sometimes stopped at bars, either for cocktails or a nightcap—something she never did. He had an easy way with people, she discovered, a capacity to strike up a conversation with strangers about sports or whatever. Once he even invited a couple he had just met to share their table.

She didn't mind. It was different. When she remarked about his casualness with people, he said, "I know. It's the midwesterner in me. We're friendlier, less reserved than you easterners. Do you mind?" She didn't and said so. It was good for her to be with people. Geoff was leading her into a larger, more adventurous world.

There was a problem, so subtle she wasn't even sure it was a problem, and she certainly didn't know how to bring it up with him. He was too attentive. There was no repeat of the episode with the waiter, yet. . . . It was hard to put a handle on. He was too attuned to everything she said, everything said to her. He involved her in his conversations or entered hers. He seemed unable to forget she was there. It was mostly all right. Who doesn't like an attentive man? Probably just the first flush of love when two people are so involved with each other. Yet she couldn't help but wonder if it had to do with her deafness. He was too conscious of her, and if the truth were admitted he did act sometimes as though he were monitoring her, grading her speech as Dr. Kovacs did. It made her a little self-conscious. Probably go away in time.

They stopped to see Doris and Derek. Irish was reluctant, then realized she was silly to want to hide Geoff away. After all, Doris had introduced them. Her witty friend's ribald teasing of them and their relationship turned out to be fun after all. Doris took her out to the kitchen where they could be alone.

"Irish, if I've ever seen an ecstatically happy woman, it's you."

She grinned. "I am, Doris. He's wonderful."

"I'll bet he's something else in bed. I envy you."

She shook her head in despair at her friend.

"Don't tell me you have a platonic relationship. You're just blooming. Only sex—real good sex—does that to a woman."

Irish blushed, couldn't help it. When they rejoined the men, she saw the look in Geoff's eyes. Relief. Was he just glad to have her there or had he been worrying about her?

On Thursday morning they drove into New York. He wanted to take his tape to his secretary, check on mail, phone calls, and such. She was delivering her Isabella painting and book jacket. It was a busy, exciting day for her. Jay Selkirk, art director at the ad agency, raved over the Isabella painting and insisted on taking her and it over to the oil company immediately. It was nervous time as a dozen executives, very stern and serious, perused her effort. She answered a few questions, mostly about the historical accuracy. Then, to her relief, somber expressions turned to smiles and her painting was greeted with enthusiasm. For over an hour she discussed others in the series. There was even talk of forming exhibits of the paintings to show to schools, women's clubs, and such.

Jay Selkirk took her to lunch and that was nice. He was in his late forties, bearded, paunchy, and rather seedy looking for the advertising business. He was divorced and, she sensed, rather lonely, although he never talked about it. A failed artist, he respected those with talent and tried to help them. Irish owed him a lot and considered him a dear friend. He was in fact one of the few people she had discussed her deafness with. Working together, he had to know. He sent wires, letters, and occasionally a messenger when he needed to communicate with her.

"You look effervescent, Irish. Are you in love?"

"Who, me?" She couldn't keep a straight face and the smile which resulted was dazzling. "Yes, madly."

"Who's the lucky fellow? Anyone I know?"

She told him about Geoff—quite a lot, really, more than she should. "I must sound like a—"

"Woman in love. I'm glad for you—and me."

"You?"

"Yeah. We got a new account, Dulche. Ever sell liqueurs?"

"Not lately."

"It ain't easy. We got an idea for a campaign. There's some talk of using photographs, but I think I can convince them art would be better. The idea is to sell brandy, crème de menthe, and such as sex objects. It seems to me photos would lean toward porno. Art would be subtler, better taste. What I'd want is something soft, very sensuous, intimate—a man and a woman, consenting adults, captured at just that moment when they decide to go to bed. You know, the way they look at each other. Maybe he's brushing her cheek with his finger. They're holding glasses of liqueur. We put the bottle down below. No message, no slogan. The art says it all. If you want to get her in bed, buy—"

"Do you think this is right for me, Jay? I've never—"

"To tell the truth, I didn't until today. But seeing you now, that lovelight in your eyes, I have an idea you'll be splendid."

She shook her head. "You're embarrassing me."

"It could be a fair-sized campaign, magazines, billboards. Wanna have a try?"

"Why not?" She promised to get some ideas together, then come to his office in the morning to meet with other agency people.

After lunch she submitted her book jacket at the editorial offices of Condor Books. It too was well received and she came away with assignments for two more and at an improved price. Wouldn't you know it? Just as a man entered her life she was becoming hopelessly busy. But the visit to Condor took too long. It was after five and she'd told Geoff she'd be at his office at four. But sometimes these things couldn't be helped, she rationalized.

Geoff's office on East 57th Street was on the sixth floor of an older building. The room she entered was more commodious and utilitarian than pretentious, paneled in mahogany, a couple of paintings of Spanish scenes, four Naugahyde chairs around a small table graced with fresh flowers and magazines. To the rear was a large desk, word processor, phone system, computer terminal, photocopier and other devices for his secretary. She was one of the more attractive women Irish had ever seen, perhaps thirty, with light brown hair, elegantly coiffed, fantastic hazel eyes expertly made up and a ripe, wide mouth. She wore a white Qiana blouse and brown skirt over a truly opulent figure. Irish was quite impressed, maybe overly so. Geoff had a sexpot for a secretary.

Irish approached the desk. "Mr. Winter, please."

Hazel eyes studied her a moment, then came a truly ravishing smile. "You must be Irish."

Irish had to admit the smile was wholly genuine, eyes adding warmth and delight. But the effect was earthy, somehow invitational. She must attract men like free beer. "Yes."

She stood up and extended a hand. "I'm Karen Chambers, Mr. Winter's secretary. He told me to expect you."

Irish took her beautifully manicured hand and felt the heartiness of the grasp. "I'm a little late."

"He's on the phone, but let's go in anyway."

Karen led her to a door behind, opening it without knocking. Geoff sat behind a huge, cluttered desk in his shirt-sleeves, tie at half mast, a phone in one hand. He looked harassed as he motioned that he'd only be a minute. It was a larger, more square room, with a big window behind the desk. Tan drapes with a green leafy pattern were open. The walls were lined with bookshelves, mostly law books, and rendered a distinct, musty odor as a library. There was a conference area to her right with a small table, couch, two chairs, maroon in color—genuine leather with some cracks from use.

"Mr. Winter tells me you're from Westport, have a dog named Sam, and are a famous artist."

"Illustrator—and hardly famous." She really was very friendly, with a natural warmth. If only she wasn't so sexy. Irish had expected Geoff's secretary to be matronly, hopefully dowdy, have gray hair at least.

"I hear you're doing a series of paintings on women rulers. Sounds very exciting."

Irish said it was and told her about it, rather noncommittally, until Geoff got off the phone. Karen excused herself and closed the door. He came from behind the desk, kissed her.

"You're late."

"Couldn't be helped. I was—"

"I worried about you."

What was in his eyes? She couldn't tell. "I'm sorry, but I can hardly phone, Geoff."

"I know." His lips pressed into a line, then broke into a smile. "You're here now. Would you like the VIP tour?"

They stayed nearly an hour. He showed her his office, some of his electronic equipment, discussed his work, then led her into adjoining offices. Most people were gone, but he introduced her to a few who remained. She loved the feel of his hand on her arm as he guided her or around her shoulders when they stopped for a more detailed look at something.

"What we're trying to do, honey, is offer a complete financial service. I'm law. Jerry Weiss is accounting. Pat Capelli insurance. Dean Rollings is a stockbroker, George Payne an investment counselor. The idea is to lure people to the sixth floor and take care of all their financial needs." He laughed. "Except making the money, that is."

"You're partners?"

"No. We're all independent, each with our own clients, but we scratch each other's backs. If I have someone who needs help with accounting, I send him to Jerry. If he needs insurance he goes to Pat, or if he wants to improve his stock portfolio, I introduce him to Dean. If he doesn't know what he wants, then it's George. And of course they refer their people to me. We also consult among ourselves to solve problems."

She smiled up at him. "I'm impressed."

Karen came in, knocking this time, to say good night. She had donned the suit jacket, freshened her makeup and looked merely ravishing. "Good to meet you, Irish. Have a nice evening, you two." Then she was gone, good nights trailing after her.

Irish looked at him, her eyes conveying mock disapproval. "That's some secretary you have."

"Karen? She's the best. Couldn't get along without her."

"I'm not talking about her typing. She's *gorgeous.*"

"Which is not bad for business. She gets more passes than a wide receiver."

"I think I'm jealous."

He smiled. "Don't be. Karen's been with me a long time. She's not had an easy life. A couple really stinko marriages, an affair worthy of a soap opera. Would you believe she has a ten-year-old son? He's her whole life. She's had it with men. She's quite bitter about them. I have a friend who calls her the praying mantis. She can be deadly to the male."

"And females?"

"I think you might get along." He grinned. "At least you don't have to worry about Karen and me. We're just friends. I took a chance on her when she was in the pits following her second marriage. One of my better decisions. She's a top drawer legal secretary today. I know a dozen guys who'd hire her away in a minute if they could." He looked at her seriously. "Feel better about her?"

"I really wasn't worried." She came to her toes and kissed him lightly. "I'm not a praying mantis."

"No, you're a honeybee."

"And you're the nectar." Again she kissed him.

His apartment was on East 73rd Street between Madison and Park, the Lenox Hill district of Manhattan. It was a modern buiding with an awning, doorman, security guard at the desk who spoke to Geoff. They went up to the ninth floor.

She really hadn't known what to expect his apartment to be like. The whole exterior wall was windows, making the place bright and more spacious than it really was. She entered a foyer. To the left was a smallish kitchen, to the right an even smaller bathroom. Straight ahead to the left and down a single stair was a narrow, rectangular living–dining room. A short hall linked that to the master bedroom, quite large and more squarish on the left. On the right, behind the bathroom, was a smaller room intended to be a second bedroom but which he used as a library, study, and den.

As he showed her around, Geoff seemed nervous. Clearly he wanted her to like his place but feared she wouldn't. She was taken aback at first, though she didn't say so, then came to see what he had done and fell in love with it. Obviously no interior decorator had ever entered the place. Instead, he had furnished it with pieces he liked or which interested him. There was a colonial dining room set, a Queen Anne couch, a French provincial hutch, a Savonarola chair, an exquisite Chippendale table, a Lay-Z-Boy recliner, a stack of Moroccan pillows, and a two-stool bar. The bedroom had a king-size bed on the floor, another recliner, TV, quadraphonic sound system, and a disorderly clutter of records and tapes. There was a large Persian rug, only slightly threadbare, in the living room and two oval hooked rugs in the bedroom. Decoration included wood carvings, an African tribal mask, pottery, and a Chinese vase with dried weeds stuck in it. The walls of the living room held several paintings with motifs from Spain, Ireland, Italy, and Scandinavia. He said he'd picked them up on his travels. In the bedroom he'd hung a bullfight poster and playbills from various movies and Broadway plays. The whole place was a mishmash of a dozen periods, devoid of motif.

"Bad, eh?"

She smiled at him. "It's you, isn't it?"

He tried to laugh. "As bad critics and dilettantes say, 'It makes a statement.' I'm not sure what."

She made another quick tour, studying the paintings particularly. None were great art. They were just interesting, nice, easy to live with. She turned to him. "I like it, Geoff. It really is you—all the things you're interested in, the way you think."

He laughed. "I didn't know I had such a cluttered mind."

"You don't, which is why you need this at day's end." She spun around, shooting her arms out to encompass the living room. "It's wonderful, a bizarre clutter, wonderful disorder, full of surprises, endlessly fascinating, yet comforting, lived in."

He was pleased, but said, "Actually I think I was a junk dealer in another life. I can't resist picking up something nobody wants, fixing it up. I keep it awhile, then sell it or give it away, find something else." He laughed. "Anything here you want—it's yours."

She came to him, locked her hands behind his neck. "I'm learning so much about you, and I like it all."

"Such as what?"

"You're a Renaissance man, interested in everything. You manage to mix Savonarola and Queen Anne with electronic gadgetry and Lay-Z-Boy. Nobody else could get away with it."

"I don't get away with it. I just don't care. What else have you learned?"

"Let's see." She raised her eyebrows in a quizzical expression. "You're a softhearted patsy."

"I'm not!"

"You don't want to be, but you are. Karen needs a job and a new start in life. You give it to her. Some forgotten bric-a-brac languishes in a junk shop. You give it a home. I'll bet you can't walk by a Salvation Army kettle without putting something in it. Heavens, you even took me in."

"Now that's different."

"How?"

He bent and kissed her, tantalizing her with his tongue, making her breathless with anticipation of what was to come. "Wow!" she said softly. "You're right. That is different."

His mouth moved toward her again, but stopped just short of its mark. She had to move her head back to see him say, "Would you like a drink, dinner, or me?"

"Let's take 'em in reverse order this time."

She sat in the kitchen, sipping wine while he phoned for dinner reservations. She wore his robe, sleeves rolled up, and felt tiny within the voluminous garment. It was rough wool with vertical black and white stripes, an Arab *djellaba* he had picked up in Tangier. All eyes for him, she watched as he hung up the wall phone, searched out his glass, and turned to her, smiling as though they shared a secret.

"Do you know that's the first time I ever slept in a bed other than my own? I mean—you know what I mean."

"So how was the strange bed?"

"Thrilling." She shook her head. "The things you do to me. I don't seem able to stop till you do."

"And I keep setting records."

He took two strides, bent over her, and kissed her raised lips. She savored it, then asked, "Will it always be this way, darling?"

"Hell, no—better. We're just getting into practice. Wait till the main event."

She grinned. "I'm sure that'll be a knockout."

"You already are a knockout. Karen was envious."

"I'll bet." She told him the exciting news of her

day, the promising appointment for the morning. "It looks like I'm going to be very busy, Geoff."

"Good. I'm happy for you."

"Really? I was hoping to be less busy, be able to spend more time with you."

He looked at her hard, squinting her eyes. "I'm not that other guy, Irish. I can entertain myself."

"But—"

"No buts, honey. One of the reasons you appeal to me so is you are a career woman, busy with your own life." He saw her disbelief. "I used to like the clinging vine type. I'll admit it. Having a woman all wrapped up in you, falling on your every word is great for the ego—for a while. Ultimately it becomes very wearing—and stultifying. I like you just the way you are. I love your success."

"Wow! What part of heaven has been reserved for you?"

"The southern part—way, way south. Will you be able to work here—some of the time, at least?"

She got up and walked into the living room to view it from a new perspective. Outside, the bright lights of New York City were a panorama. She felt him come beside her and slip his arm around her. "I don't see why not. There's plenty of light. What about Sam? I'm sure he's miserable in the kennel."

"Sam can come. Manhattan's the world's largest kennel. I'll get a pooper scooper."

"Sam's a very private dog. He'll be offended."

"Actually I wished he were here today. I worried about you, figured Sam would have helped."

His words jolted her. "You're not serious!"

"There's a lot of crazy stuff in this city—maniac cab drivers, police chases, fire engines. You can't hear horns and sirens. Isn't Sam trained to warn you of that?"

She was annoyed and made no effort to hide it. "Do you think I need Sam to cross the street? I've been doing it for years, Geoff."

He shook his head, exhaling deeply. She could see it. "Okay, okay, it was a dumb thing to say."

"But you thought it. Did you really worry about me?"

Another sigh. "Yes, but I shouldn't, should I?"

"No, you shouldn't." She felt her annoyance disintegrating. "I get along fine. In fact, I love being in the city."

"I know. I'm sorry. Look, there are things about you I have to get used to. Just give me a chance."

"I thought I was. What were we just doing in the bedroom?" she asked, smiling seductively.

"Something we both enjoy quite a bit," he replied with a grin before he scooped her up in his arms. He lifted her chin with his forefinger. "I love you, Irish O'Brien."

"May that always remain as remarkable as it is right now."

"It will."

They went out for dinner to Trattoria Luigi, a small Italian restaurant in Greenwich Village, reached by cab. Geoff was effusively greeted by Luigi, a short, rotund man, and his equally substantial wife, Maria. Apparently Geoff was a regular. Irish had trouble with Luigi's accent at first, but his florid gestures helped and she was able to understand how glad he was to see them and that she was *bellissima*. They were seated at a table. Luigi brought Chianti and menus.

"I come here often."

She smiled. "That's obvious. I thought you were a relative for a moment."

"I almost am. Do you like it?"

She looked around. Red and white checked tablecloths, dripping candles in wine bottles, Italian scenes on the wall. "Yes, very much. A touch of Roma."

"Sorrento, actually. The food is Neapolitan and very good. Were you able to understand Luigi? His accent is so thick even I have trouble."

It annoyed her. Couldn't he forget her deafness? But she let it go. "Most of it, I think. His gestures tell their own story."

They ordered, veal parmigiana for him, ravioli for her. When it came, Luigi was there asking how everything was. She told him it was delicious.

"*Signor* Winter, maya I speaka to you—privately." A wide gesture with his hands indicated his request was of no great importance. "After you and the *signorina bellissima* hava eaten."

"Of course." When Luigi departed, Geoff said to her, "I help him with his taxes sometimes."

She smiled. "You help him, you help me. Do you ever charge?"

"Oh, indeed."

They ate, talking about the food, his trips to Italy. Going abroad on business was clearly one of the rewards of his profession. But she noticed he was distracted, a little annoyed, and kept glancing over her shoulder. Finally he said, "That damn table back of you. Too loud. Can't hear yourself think."

She looked around. The place had filled up while they were there. The table just behind her was occupied by a half dozen men in business suits. They were very animated.

"Mafia, I think—and drunk."

"They don't bother me, Geoff."

"Another advantage of deafness."

Her only visible reaction was to purse her lips. When they finished eating, Geoff excused himself and went to the cash register in front to confer with Luigi. Her back was to him. She sat quietly, sipping her wine, pondering what to her was a growing problem. Geoff couldn't forget her deafness. It intruded constantly, changing his behavior, at least in public, and making her aware of her own limitation. Should she just let it go and hope he got over it? Or should she say something? But what, and when?

She felt a rough hand on her right shoulder. It startled her and she turned. A young, handsome man stood above her, but the hand came from the man directly behind her. She turned to him. He was a bit older, obviously quite drunk. She saw his mouth and knew he was speaking loudly.

"All I asked was to borrow your extra chair for my friend. You ain't usin' it."

"I'm sorry, I—"

"Do you think the chair belongs to you or somethin'?"

"I was distracted. Of course you—"

Geoff was there, grabbing the man, jerking his hand away. "Take your hand off her."

"All I asked was to use the chair. Is she deaf or somethin'?"

He grabbed the man by his suit front and pulled him out of the chair. "That's exactly what she is. She didn't hear you."

Irish stood up, shocked by the violence in Geoff. She gaped at him, saw the man knock Geoff's hand away and raise his fist. He was restrained by other men at the table, all of whom had stood up.

An older man, perhaps in his fifties, with salt and pepper hair, very dignified, said, "I apologize for Gino. He has had too much vino, I fear."

Geoff's anger still flared. "He's not going to talk to her that way."

"He was most rude. Again, I apologize." He turned to her, his eyes placating, and bowed his head. "Forgive us, please. I will teach my friend better manners." He glared momentarily at Gino, then smiled at Geoff. "Permit me to order you another bottle of wine."

Irish could bear it no longer. She picked up her purse and stalked out of the trattoria into the street, looking frantically for a cab. She saw one with a dome light, waved, watched it stop. Geoff arrived in time to crawl in after her and tell the cab to go to 73rd and Park.

Huddled in the corner of the seat as far away from him as she could get, Irish sensed he was speaking to her but kept her face averted, staring out at the passing streets. Depression, anger, a sense of humiliation, and gross disappointment in Geoff Winter all vied for command of her mind. How could he? What kind of a man was he? She felt him touch her arm, trying to get her to look at him. She would not. Couldn't read his lips in the darkened cab if she wanted to.

She alighted from the cab by herself and stalked into his apartment house, ignoring both the doorman and security guard who said something to her. The elevator was not empty, carrying another couple up from the underground garage, so Geoff had to keep his distance. She wasn't about to look at him anyway. At the door to his apartment she fumbled for the key he had given her. He was quicker, opening the door. She walked past him and headed for the bedroom, tossing her overnighter on the bed to repack the few things she had brought.

He made her look at him, turning her, hands

holding her head, his thumbs at the corner of her eyes. "I was only trying to protect you."

Her anger flared out of her mouth. "You call that protection? Almost getting into a fistfight?"

"Nobody hit anyone."

"No thanks to you!" She struggled, pushing at his arms, trying to get away from him.

"I couldn't let him talk to you that way."

"So you embarrassed *me* instead. Thanks a lot." Her voice ladled sarcasm.

"Irish, the man put—"

"Don't blame it on him. You're the one. I could have handled him. He was just a drunk in a restaurant. I've been in far worse situations. But, no, Geoff Winter has to get on his high horse, charge over, pick a fight, and—" she shook her head so violently she freed herself from his grasp "—and make a total *ass* out of himself—me along with him."

Her words had stung him. She saw his anger rise and his inner struggle with it. "Do you really mean that?"

"You better believe I do. There were a dozen different ways to handle it—all of them better."

He seemed to weigh her words, then accept them as truth. He nodded his head several times. "I'm sorry, Irish. It won't happen again."

"You're damn right it won't." She bent over the suitcase. "I'm going back to Westport. There's a late train." When she started for the closet to get her dress he was there. She had to look at him.

"Don't go. I said I'm sorry. Can't I be allowed one mistake?"

She eyed him a long moment, her anger still ripe within her. "It's not just one mistake, Geoff. Every time I go out with you it's the same thing. This was just a little worse."

"What d'you mean?"

"You can't forget I'm deaf. It's constantly on your mind. You're wondering what I heard, explaining what was said, listening to my every word. I feel like I'm being graded by a teacher. You smother me. You make me self-conscious—and I haven't felt that way in years." She saw his lips firm into a line, the hurt in his eyes. "I get along fine, or at least I did till I met you."

She watched him turn away and lean over the chest of drawers on outstretched arms. He looked so dejected and she could see him shaking. In a moment he turned back to her. "You're right. I've not been acting naturally. But it's only because I care about you. I love you, Irish."

"Too much."

"I thought you loved me."

She shook her head. "I do." Hot tears came to her eyes, quite unwanted. "But it's not going to work, is it? It's better I go now . . . before—"

"I asked for a chance, Irish. It hasn't been a week yet. Not long enough." He came to her, hands on her upper arms. "I can change, honey. Believe me I can. I will."

She shook her head, unwilling to believe him. "Everybody's got something wrong with them: color blind, tone deaf, poor sense of direction. They have two left feet, maybe fall down a lot, maybe they wear glasses. Maybe they can't spell or read slowly or flunk multiplication. Lots of people have accents, mispronounce words, use poor grammar."

"I know."

"You never notice *them*. Your friend Luigi is all

right. But I'm not. I'm deaf—a *curiosity.*" She shook with anger and revulsion. "You make me feel like a *cripple.* I—I can't . . . *live* with that."

His response was to take her in his arms, holding her close, the heat of his body melting her anger. She felt his hand moving over her back, soothing her. It went on a long time. Finally he moved away and she saw his moving lips.

"I won't let you go, Irish. I can't. I'm going to do better. I promise. You'll see."

She wanted to believe. With her whole heart she did.

"Besides—" his lips spread into a smile "—you have an important appointment in the morning. No sense in going to Westport tonight."

She searched his face with her eyes, twin blue pools of immeasurable depth, seeking confirmation of what she wanted, hoped was true. "Just treat me as you do when we're alone—accept me, ignore me, stop worrying about me."

"I know. Just love you."

"I want to be like everyone else, Geoff. Deafness is only part of my life, not the whole of it."

"Yes." He nodded, several times, his face very serious. "How on earth can you love a sap like me."

SEVEN

Irish was having a hard time with the third painting of women rulers. Jay Selkirk said the oil company wanted a modern ruler. They shouldn't all be historical figures. That meant Margaret Thatcher. Her most notable achievement was the Falkland Islands War, but that posed a problem. How to portray her? Irish felt she could hardly put the prime minister on the deck of a warship. She hadn't actually done any fighting.

After a lot of discussion, a decision was made to create a scene in which Mrs. Thatcher was briefing Queen Elizabeth II—two rulers for the price of one —standing before a map of the South Atlantic. To the side would be a couple of war scenes with ships and planes, creating a montage effect. Irish wasn't entirely happy with it, but nobody could come up with a better idea.

Her opinion as she looked at the half finished painting: adequate, but not great. It lacked the momentous feeling that the first two paintings had. Probably couldn't be helped. The Falkland Islands War was a minor skirmish between two second-rate powers at best. And why did war have to be used, anyway? Women rulers had done a lot better things than make war.

She felt Sam stir at her feet, reached down, and petted him. "You know what the trouble is, darlin'? I'm just not involved with this painting. It's too

114

static. And I don't really care whether Margaret Thatcher and the queen ever laid eyes on each other. Oh, well. Can't be helped. And who said every painting had to be a masterpiece?"

She watched Sam cock his ears and turn his head as though trying to understand her. "Maybe the problem's not this painting, but me. Maybe I'm too in love, too wrapped up in you know who to get really interested in prime ministers and queens." She didn't really think so. The sketch she had made for the Dulche liqueurs ad had been fun. Yes, but it had been a romantic scene between two lovers. "Face it, Sam. I'm in love—and isn't that nice? I know, it's nothing special to you, you unromantic beast, you." She laughed. "Maybe if we didn't shut you out of the bedroom. . . ." Another laugh. "You're too young and naive for that."

Two weeks after "the quarrel," as she thought of it, all was bliss. Geoff truly was making a real effort to be more relaxed with her in public—and succeeding. She felt more comfortable with him when they went out. Oh, there were occasional lapses, moments of overprotectiveness, but he usually caught himself. Indeed, his tendency to mother-hen her had become something of a joke between them.

She glanced at the clock. Quarter till six. A couple of hours at least before he got there. She grimaced. Another problem, and she really didn't know what to do about it. She knew he wasn't wild about driving out to Westport every evening—and he hated the train even more. But staying at his apartment really hadn't worked out. She had taken only minimal equipment into New York and considered the time spent there mostly a waste as far as work went. Face it, she accomplished lots more right here. Selfish of her, no doubt. An imposition on Geoff. Thank God, he was a good sport about it.

She stripped off her smock and hung it over the easel, provoking Sam to throw a tizzy at the door. "Want a run, do you? Well, my friend, I'm not at your beck and call anymore. I've a man to think of. The least you can do is let me think about feeding him." She went to the refrigerator and studied the meat keeper, trying to make up her mind. Pot roast. That ought to please a meat and potatoes man—if he didn't OD on cholesterol. Just had to do something about his diet. She braised the roast in her Dutch oven, then set it for simmer. The vegetables could be added later. Only then did she take Sam for his mad dash on the beach, following up with a swim.

By eight o'clock she was all dressed up waiting for Geoff. The evenings had turned a little cooler after Labor Day, and she wore a long cotton skirt with a floral pattern in it and a dressy pink sweater with a cowl neck. Very feminine. She was pleased to discover Geoff appreciated a touch of elegance. It was difficult in the cottage because there was no dining room, but she could look the part herself. Indeed, of all the changes he had wrought in her, the most apparent was her heightened regard for her appearance. Gone was the sloppy attire, at least when he was around. She wanted to look beautiful for him and invested in appropriate lingerie, heels, and dresses. Hair curlers, lumpy robes, and old shirts were a guaranteed way to make a man lose interest —not that he showed any signs of it.

When he hadn't come by eight-thirty, she worked a bit on the Thatcher painting, then remembered the pot roast, going to the kitchen to turn it off. "Hope he likes his meat overdone," she said to

Sam. By ten o'clock she had eaten her own dinner and was reading the manuscript for the next book jacket. Another thriller, this one set in Saudi Arabia. A plot to kill King Suad and throw the Middle East into greater turmoil than it already was.

In truth she knew she was glancing at the clock too often. No sense in worrying about him. He was held up, that's all. Somebody probably showed up from out of town like the last time. He'd worked late, then came drinks and dinner with a client. Couldn't be helped. She'd told him then to stay in the city. No sense in driving out to Westport so late. By eleven-forty, after the TV news, she was sure that was what he had done and decided to go to bed. She was outside on the porch in her robe, letting Sam tend to his leg lifting, when Geoff drove in.

He looked weary; fatigue was etched around his eyes. She made him a drink, then watched him plop onto a couch as though it were the last act of his life. She had never seen him so tired.

"Awful traffic for this hour. There was an accident on the turnpike which held me up a half hour. Seemed forever—just sitting there, waiting, unable to move."

"You shouldn't have driven out at this hour."

He laid his head back against the cushion and closed his eyes. "I know, but I wanted to see you. Figured you wouldn't know where I was—and worry."

"Well, I didn't. I knew you must have worked late. Did you?"

"Yes. Tim Donaldson showed up from the West Coast with a client—Kevin O'Neill, the actor. Heard of him?"

She smiled. "He's the hunk with the blond hair,

117

brown eyes, and an Irish name. Only trouble is there's never been an Irishman with that coloring."

"I don't care if he's red, white, and blue with purple spots. He's looking for tax shelters, setting up a trust fund. Gonna be some bucks in it for me." He sighed. "I just couldn't get away sooner."

"Did you eat?" She saw him say he had. *Just make him another drink*, she thought. She did and brought it to him.

"I sure wish I could've phoned you. It makes it so much worse—knowing I'm late, worrying about your worrying. There's no way to let you know."

His words disturbed her. Somehow all this was now her fault. If she weren't deaf and could use a phone, he wouldn't have had to drive out here late at night. "I told you I didn't worry."

He studied her. "You didn't? That could've been me in the accident."

"I suppose, but there's nothing I can do about that, is there? No sense in worrying." She smiled. "Besides, I figure you can look after yourself."

He seemed to weigh that statement. "Makes sense—except for one thing. I'd like to talk to you at least once a day, find out how your day went, share mine with you. If I were out of town that's what I'd do. Doesn't everyone?"

She truly felt defensive now. He was right, but her deafness made that utterly impossible. It was a complication in their lives which had never occurred to her. She squatted before him and slipped off his loafers. It was an unconscious act, unwilled. Was she trying to make up to him for her deficiency? "You could have phoned Mrs. Harrington next door and left a message you were staying over. Didn't I give you the number?"

"I left it in the office and couldn't remember it."

118

"Let's fix that." She went to the kitchen, jotted the number on a notepad, tore it off, and returned to him. "Here. Put this in your wallet. You'll have it with you the next time."

He took it and slipped it in his pants pocket. "I still don't like to call the neighbors, Irish."

Irritation welled within her. She couldn't squelch it. "Then don't. I'm a big girl. I don't have to know what you're doing every second."

He stared at her. "Little Miss Independence. You don't need anyone."

She bit at her lip. "Yes, I do. I need you. You must know that."

He seemed not to have heard her. "I'm committed to you, Irish. I'm involved with you, your life. I care what happens to you, and I want you to care about my life. People change, but slowly, subtly. If you and I don't communicate those changes, we're going to grow apart. That's what ruins most marriages."

Again she knew he was right. Her repeated nods affirmed that. But she smiled. "I had a very dull day. I didn't meet any movie stars." She saw him react. He had been serious. Her attempt at wit was not funny to him. "I'll be serious. I know what you're saying. You're right. We do have a communication problem when we're apart. I don't know what to do about it except try to make up for it when we're together. I'm just—" She hesitated, sighing deeply. "I'm just sorry you had to drive out here. It makes me feel guilty."

"Then don't. I want to be here. Let's not fight anymore, okay?"

She smiled. "This isn't fighting. I'll let you know when it is." She leaned over and kissed him, lingering, felt his hand within her robe. Delectable sensa-

119

tions followed. "Aha, so the real truth comes out now."

He pulled her down into his lap. "Never could fool you."

The letter from Jay Selkirk arrived Friday morning by overnight express mail. Irish opened it and read with delight. Jay liked her drawing for the Dulche ad and wanted her to come in today after lunch for a meeting. "Sam, darlin', you're about to become a rich mutt. Don't spend the money foolishly." Then she thought of Geoff. That would work out. She'd take the one o'clock train. There'd be plenty of time to stop at his office and make plans to meet later. They could drive back to Westport together for the weekend.

The train was late and there wasn't a blessed thing to be done about it. Oh, she could have changed her plan and driven in, but the train was expected any minute, and she hated to have two cars in the city. She and Geoff wouldn't be able to drive back out together. When the train finally came, it was delayed even more by rail construction near Harrison. It was after three when she reached Grand Central, which didn't leave her any time to run up to 57th Street. She'd have Jay's secretary phone Geoff with a message.

That didn't work out. No one answered at Geoff's office, not even Karen. Maybe he'd closed early for the weekend. Better phone the Harringtons and leave a message. Then she remembered. The Harringtons were away. She shrugged. Couldn't be helped. She'd catch up with Geoff sooner or later.

Jay was enthusiastic about her submission; everyone was. She had drawn a couple, quite beautiful people, just rising from a candlelight dinner. The female wore an off-the-shoulder gown of gold lamé which glistened in the candlelight. There was surprise, delight, and anticipation in her eyes as she turned toward the loving eyes and eager mouth of the man. He was just setting down his snifter of brandy to free both his hands. Hers were caught in mid-descent.

"It's perfect, Irish, as I knew it would be. It carries the whole message. Drink Dulche liqueurs and get the sweet life."

"Or be overcome with lust." She laughed.

"How's your love life?"

She saw his grin. "Very loving."

"I can tell from your work." He stood up. "C'mon. Got some people waiting."

The conference was prolonged, a dozen people around a long table brainstorming the Dulche ad campaign. Everyone contributed ideas: Have them in bed reaching for a glass of liqueur on the nightstand; cuddled by the fireplace, glass in hand; on a moonlit tropical balcony, holding tall, frosty glasses. Another man suggested foreign backgrounds, the Parthenon, the Leaning Tower of Pisa, a Caribbean isle. This would suggest the origins of the liqueurs: the world and romance in a bottle. Irish took notes. She was having a hard, mentally exhausting time with so many people talking at once, but she managed.

Afterward she and Jay Selkirk met with the agency vice-president about her remuneration. Five grand a drawing. At that price she could hardly refuse their invitation to a cocktail, nor did she want to.

She missed the express train and had to take a slower one. It was nearly nine o'clock when she arrived home to encounter an angry Geoff Winter.

121

"I'm sorry. I tried to phone and leave a message. There was no answer."

"I closed the office early, gave Karen the afternoon off. I've been here since two-thirty, Irish."

She saw the coldness in his eyes. "And in a stew."

"Dammit, Irish. I had no idea where you were. Nobody home next door. Doris didn't know. I drove all over town looking for your car, even called the deaf school in Hartford."

She bristled. So stupid! All this fuss! "I was in New York. Couldn't you figure that out?"

"I finally did. I found your car over by the station. As far as I was concerned it only made it worse. Dammit, Irish, why didn't you leave me a note telling me where you were?"

She sighed, trying to subdue her rising anger. "I should have. I would have if I'd known there was going to be all this fuss. I thought I'd meet you in the city and—"

"You *thought!*"

He had hurled the word at her. An insult! She was an idiot to him. Still she struggled to control her anger. "It's just a misunderstanding, Geoff. The train was late, I missed you at your office, the conference ran late. Couldn't be helped." She watched him, saw his angry petulance, and sought to ameliorate it. She smiled. "Aren't you going to ask what I was doing in New York?"

"Frankly I don't much care."

That did it. "You're awful! The only thing that matters is *you—your* business, *your* life. *You* had to wait. *You* didn't know where I was. At least I know where I stand with you."

She saw him expel his breath in a long sigh. "I know I shouldn't be angry, but I can't help it. What I really am is glad to see you, know you're all right."

Her anger exploded now. "Why don't you get a dog like Sam? Put *him* on a leash. I'm not your pet. I'm not at your beck and call. I don't heel and roll over at your command, sit at your feet, and lick your hand." She saw her words striking deep, hurting him. "You said you wanted an independent woman, a career woman. Clearly you don't. You want an ornament for your life. Go find a clinging vine."

"That's not fair and you know it. Is it so wrong to wonder where you are and worry about you?"

"Yes! You know what the problem is as well as I do. It's the second time this week we've fought about it. If I weren't deaf this wouldn't happen. You wouldn't worry where I was. You wouldn't give it a passing thought. But I *am* deaf. And there's not a blessed thing I can do about it." She saw him interrupting but paid no attention. "You think I'm a cripple. I can't get through life without you. I'm going to get run over by a car, fall into a manhole, wander around like a lost child. I don't know what goes on in that crazy head of yours. But I do know this: I can't live with it."

She saw him staring at her, visibly shaking as he sought to control his anger. Finally he said, "Is this a real fight?"

She nodded. "I think so."

"You're good at it." He turned and snatched up his sports jacket from a chair back. "Let's go eat. I'm starved."

They drove to Allen's Clamhouse by the water. The process of driving there, being seated, and ordering dissipated her anger but left her depressed. For the first time she faced a painful fact, one she'd known all along, even predicted. It wasn't going to work with Geoff. Love wasn't enough. The obstacles were too great.

"We have a problem, don't we?"

She looked at him, biting at her lip. "I don't want to quarrel any more."

"Nor I. Say what's on your mind."

She hesitated, then plunged ahead. "I don't think I have a problem, Geoff—at least none I haven't had for a long time and adjusted to. You're the one with the problem, not me."

He nodded several times, as though letting her words sink in. "I love you, Irish."

"And I love you—with all my heart." She pursed her lips. "But it's not enough, is it?"

"Yes, it is. Love is always enough. We can find a way." He smiled. "I mean, I can find a way. Do you want to try?"

"I do, of course, but—" She shook her head. "But I don't see how."

"I've been thinking. I honestly don't believe the problem is what you think it is. The problem is we are two people, busy, successful, involved in separate lives. We'd have that if you . . ." He let his voice trail off, obviously not wanting to refer to her impairment.

She did. "If I weren't deaf? Perhaps it is part of the trouble."

"Yes, part. But mostly it is living in two places, Westport and New York, an hour apart."

"And no telephone."

"Exactly. You have to admit there's a communication problem. I can't let you know when my plans change. You can't let me know what you're up to. That's what all this is really about, Irish."

She was anything but convinced, but said, "Perhaps."

"Problems are to be solved. This one can be— easily. We have to live one place or the other."

She looked out at the water, Long Island Sound. A rising moon reflected on it. When she turned back to him she said, "Which means your place, doesn't it? Mine's too small. And the communication problem would still exist. You want me to move into New York with you?"

"Yes, that's what I'd like."

Again she looked away, out at the moon on the water, then scanned diners at the other tables, finally coming back to him.

"If you don't want to, say so."

She saw his penetrating eyes, the lovely mouth, so desirable. "I'm very discouraged, Geoff—about us."

"It's going to work. Don't think otherwise."

"I want it to. I want to be with you."

"We have had happiness, haven't we?"

"Oh yes, lots—wonderful lots." She sighed, pressed her lips together. "Geoff, I can't give up my home, the life I've built. I'm not sure enough of you —of us—for that."

"Nobody's asking you to. By all means keep your cottage. We'll spend weekends there, any other time we can."

She thought about that, what moving into the city would entail. "To be honest, I don't get much work done at your place. And I have to." She told him her good news of the day, only it didn't seem so good now.

"That's wonderful, Irish. I'm so happy for you. You're going great guns."

She ignored his praise. "If I move all the stuff I need into 73rd Street, then my time in Westport will be wasted."

"You sure are fighting it. Couldn't you duplicate your stuff, be outfitted at both places?"

"I suppose. I do need some new things anyway."

"I'll happily pay for it."

"You needn't." She looked away, as though the view of the Sound could relieve the dejection she felt. She was aroused by his taking her hand across the table. She turned to him.

"Say whatever you're thinking, Irish. You owe that much to me."

She nodded. "All right. Aren't we just postponing the inevitable, Geoff?"

"The breakup of you and me? Is that what you mean?"

"Yes."

"It'll never happen. I love you, you love me. We're two independent people, yet somehow we belong together. Kahlil Gibran wrote it best in *The Prophet:* We're the strings of the lute. We stand alone, yet we quiver with the same music. Irish, we can never make music without each other."

She smiled. "That's nice."

"I believe it. That's what marriage is to me. I never liked that candle ceremony they do at weddings—you know, two people light a single candle, then blow the originals out. That's wrong. Nobody loses their identity in marriage. Both candles continue to burn, making a brighter light."

"I never thought of it that way."

"Think of it now, Irish. Think of marrying me. I mean it. You and I both know it's going to come to that."

She had to look away. His eyes were too intense, too probing. "Geoff, my darling, declarations of love and marriage, however fervently meant, do not make problems go away. You know that."

"Yes. I want you to be sure. Let's solve whatever

126

problems there are first. But let's do it together. Will you at least try New York?"

She studied his handsome face, as though noticing it for the first time. Finally she smiled. "You really are nice looking."

"I'm serious."

"So am I. I'm thinking a girl would be a fool to let you get away without having done all she could to keep you. Yes, I'll move into New York. I'll try my hardest to make you happy and be happy myself. I want it to work. I want us." He sat there beaming, his eyes full of love. "There's only one problem."

"Now what?"

"You get to tell Sam he's going to be a city dog."

He laughed. "Then let's eat up and go home and tell him—along with other things."

After an atrocious start, the weekend turned into a time of love and laughter. It was as if, frightened by the close call that had nearly torn them apart, they clung to each other with particular fervor. Sunday afternoon they moved Irish into New York, along with much of her clothes and art paraphernalia, and Sam too. She left her car behind in the Parkins's garage, figuring she'd have no use for it in the city. Irish knew she was taking a big step moving in with Geoff, and on that sunny Sunday she had no doubts that it was a step in the right direction.

EIGHT

Sam jumped up, nudged her with his nose, and ran across the room. Hard at work at her drawing board set up in the window of Geoff's apartment, she knew what it meant. Sam had heard the bell on the teletype, warned her. She turned, saw the blinking red light, then followed Sam. "Good dog. Let's see what the message is."

Geoff had installed it within the first week of her move to New York, surprising her, making a big production of it. "I think we just solved our communication problem," he'd said. "Why didn't I think of it before?" The teletype linked the apartment with his office. Over it they could exchange messages at will, alerting each other of delays and changed plans. It was wonderful. She thought of it as "that blessed instrument," and kept among her keepsakes his first message over it: I LOVE YOU.

Smiling, she watched the message appear on the roll of paper: GOT FREEBIES FOR *DEATH OF A SALESMAN* WITH DUSTIN HOFFMAN. WANT TO GO?

She sat at the keyboard, typed: TONIGHT?

SORRY. I SHOULD HAVE SAID THAT. YES, TONIGHT.

It was like magic to her. She could visualize him at his machine. It was almost like talking to him. YES, DARLING. I'D LOVE TO.

128

GOOD. MEET YOU AT SARDI'S AT 7. DON'T FORGET YOUR BIG EYES.

She smiled. *Big eyes* was his term for binoculars. She used them to help read lips at plays. It worked surprisingly well. Geoff mouthed to her words said offstage or by people with their backs to the audience, and she was able to follow most dramas. It had opened up a whole vista of fun for her. They even went to musicals, concerts, and opera sometimes. She loved being there and swore she could *feel* the music she couldn't hear.

She brought her fingers to the keyboard. I WON'T FORGET. I'M TAKING SAM FOR HIS RUN. SEE YOU AT 7. BYE.

Yes, a blessed instrument. It had all but solved their communication problems. She and Geoff could stay in touch now. She even used it to give him a grocery list to bring home—just like a regular housewife.

She glanced off to her right, then shook her head. Fall had passed into winter, then a new year, and she still wasn't used to the absence of her mother's clock. Now she looked at her wristwatch. Ten to five. "Better go now, hadn't we, darling." She reached down and petted Sam, then bent lower to hug him. "If you don't get some exercise your cabin fever will become terminal." Sam was clearly unhappy. In the apartment he spent most of his time lying or sitting by the window, staring out as though trying to glimpse the life he had loved. Exercise was a huge problem. She had to keep him on a leash, which he hated. She tried to run him in Central Park every day, but it wasn't the same. Too many people misunderstood his friendliness and were afraid. When the weather was bad, she took to running him and herself up and down nine flights of stairs in the building. It was good exercise, but hardly fun. "Too much ice outside, darlin'. I'm afraid it's the stairs for us again today." She went to the bedroom to change.

Irish felt that at best she could give only mixed reviews to city life. She loved the energy, the feeling that things were happening even when they weren't. And the variety. All those people, each so different, each struggling to find vitality in conditions which were unnatural at best and often extremely difficult. Just finding space and privacy on crowded subways, buses, sidewalks, elevators, and stores required great ingenuity and forbearance. New Yorkers, she noticed, never knew their neighbors or spoke to strangers, indeed hardly looked at them. Out-of-towners thought them cold and unfriendly, failing to understand the need for privacy or observe that in their homes and neighborhoods they were extremely outgoing and gregarious.

It seemed to Irish that the sidewalks of New York were a stage on which ordinary people acted out the events of their lives as vignettes—bag ladies, drunks, aspiring models, striving yuppies, tired cops, quarreling couples, the self-important, celebrities trying to be incognito, street musicians, downright crazies, and all those living out their lives in unquiet desperation. She loved the city as a melting pot, all the races, every nationality. She and Geoff had begun a culinary round-the-world tour, endeavoring to sample every ethnic cuisine in New York. So far they had braved a dozen different ones, surely an act of valor for a meat and potatoes man.

She loved the elegance. This play tonight would be great fun. There were so many things to do—museums, art galleries, exhibits, sporting events. She had become a hockey fan. On the plus side, too, she was getting a lot of work done. She had uninterrupted days, lots of time. And there could be no doubt proximity to art directors made it easy to drum up work. She insisted on contributing to expenses and spent more money on clothes and such than she had ever dreamed about. Yet her bank account still grew, creating a tax problem for Geoff to solve.

But there were negatives, lots of them. She felt cooped up in his apartment and often shared Sam's cabin fever. Going out into the streets, shopping or just for a walk, didn't relieve it. Concrete canyons. Even Central Park was just a wider canyon. Often she felt smothered and had a hard time waiting for the weekend and the openness and fresh air and privacy of her beach at Westport. When they couldn't go for some reason, she was downright miserable and irritable.

Both she and Sam metamorphosed when they reached Westport Friday evening. Sam was in doggie heaven and she felt rejuvenated. There was no doubt in her mind Westport was home to her, New York a place she spent time. She even extended the weekend through Monday, driving up to Hartford for her therapy, spending the afternoon in the cottage before coming to the city in the evening.

She put on her running shoes, noting Sam's impatience. "Know what our problem is, love? You and I are becoming schizophrenic. We're living in two places, two different lives. We need a nest, Sam, someplace to call home." She headed for the door. "C'mon, before you burst your bladder."

She ran down nine flights of stairs with him, then walked him a few blocks on his leash while he relieved himself, then ran back up to the apartment. She figured Sam made the trip at least three times because of all his running back while she caught up. Finally inside, panting heavily, she said, "Wanna do it again?" then laughed. "Boy, am I glad you can't really understand me."

There was a message for her on the teleprinter. KAREN HERE. HOW ABOUT LUNCH TOMORROW? Irish smiled. Loneliness was a problem for her. She missed Doris and her other Westport friends, their dropping by, the impulsive lunches and tennis games. Geoff understood and did his best to make her feel welcome among his friends. This was not altogether easy, for cocktail parties, so often a social outlet in New York, were difficult for her. Often she had a couple over for dinner or they went out to eat. They were nice people, interesting, sometimes fun, but in truth she didn't feel close to any of them. Two people were special. Jay Selkirk was completely supportive, both professionally and personally. He was truly a decent human being who was a little lonely, a little out of step with the world, somehow unfulfilled. The other was Karen Chambers.

She sat at the keyboard. ARE YOU THERE, KAREN?

In a moment a reply came. YES. BACK FROM YOUR RUN WITH SAM? HOW WAS IT?

WE DID THE STAIRS. UGH! I'D LOVE LUNCH. WHERE?

I'LL LET YOU KNOW IN THE MORNING. I'M BEING SUMMONED. BYE.

Irish smiled at the machine as though she were smiling at Karen. Few things in her life had surprised her as much as her friendship with Geoff's secretary. It began one lonely day when Irish teletyped a message to Geoff asking if he were free for lunch. Karen messaged back that he was in court and had a lunch date, but she was free. Irish hesitated over the keyboard. Why not?

That day and on subsequent occasions she discovered Karen to be a warm, outgoing, caring person whose lush sensuality created only problems for her. She attracted men simply by existing. They stared at her, made passes, felt compelled to touch her or at least try to. Irish was flabbergasted and said so. "I don't know how you stand it."

"I'm used to it—or tell myself I am. Tell me, Irish, do you notice anything I do to cause it?"

"You could try gunnysacks, muumuus, and hair curlers." She laughed. "You're just lucky, I guess."

"Hardly. It's not so much that I mind the attention. It's just that—" She hesitated, lifting her wineglass, but not drinking. Her eyes seemed troubled. "I guess I might as well say it. I seem to bring out the worst in men. He seems a nice guy. We go out to dinner, maybe the theater. But to him that's just the prelude. He spent money, therefore he's bought a ticket to—" She shrugged. "There's always a hassle."

"He comes down with terminal lust."

"Worse than that. Two husbands and a lover have beaten me."

"You're kidding!"

"No, I'm not. It's the truth. I've had black eyes, cut lip, bruises, the whole bit."

Irish shook her head. "That's awful!"

She nodded. "Yeah, Karen the punching bag. And I don't know why. These weren't tough guys. My first husband was an account executive with a leading stockbroker, the second a computer salesman. The lover was an ad executive. Big bucks. I don't think any of them ever swatted a fly, but they did me. Can you figure it out?"

Again Irish shook her head. "I don't know. It's beyond my experience."

"I should hope so." She smiled. "Geoff wouldn't lift a finger. He adores you. I've never seen him so happy. You're very good for him."

Irish beamed. "I am lucky, I know."

"Yes, you are. Don't lose him."

"I don't plan to." She hesitated, wanting to say something, then thinking better of it.

"Did you have something you wanted to ask?"

"No, I—"

"Just in case you wanted to ask if there has ever been anything between Geoff and me, the answer is no." She smiled. "And I really don't know why. He's attractive enough. I guess it's because he's the one man other than my father—and I'm not entirely sure of him—who never came on to me. Geoff's given me a good job, a nice salary, sent me to night school, helped me gain independence. Believe me, that's important to a girl like me. I wouldn't give it up—even if he ever did come on to me." Again she smiled. "You're safe with me."

Irish nodded. Somehow she was terribly pleased to know all that.

"You were helping me figure out why men turn into Muhammad Ali with me."

"Yes. I really don't know. What do the men say?"

"My husbands? They're sorry, can't understand what came over them, never happen again. But it did."

Shaking her head in disbelief, Irish said, "Maybe it has something to do with the way you look. You're so attractive, so built. Face it, you're just plain sexy."

"I'm really not, Irish. It isn't that great for me. Quite honestly, I'm just as happy without it."

"Could that be the problem? You look so sexy. You're every man's walking fantasy. He gets big ideas—"

"And when it doesn't turn out the way he wants, he's disappointed, angry, blames me for not coming on to him and—whammo!—he belts me. I never thought of it that way."

"And it's probably a lot of poppycock. Why don't you ask a therapist?"

"Not worth the trouble. I'm happy the way I am. Just my son Ricky and me against the world. Who needs a love life?"

Irish went into the bedroom, stripped off her sweat suit, then wavered between a shower and a bath, electing the latter. As she soaked, her mind returned to Karen Chambers. There could be no doubt she filled a void in her life. They saw each other often, lunches, drinks waiting for Geoff, or at the office. In between they chattered over the teletype. It puzzled Irish at first why she was so drawn to the sexy-looking secretary. Then she realized they were kindred spirits. Karen might have all her senses intact, but her life was impaired by an effect upon men which denied her happiness. Yes. There were all kinds of handicaps. Nice to have her for a friend—a confidante, really. She felt closer to Karen Chambers than she did to Doris, Dr. Kovacs, or anyone else. Even Geoff Winter? She smiled. That was a different closeness.

Irish loved the play. She was moved to both tears and laughter, and she had a sense of observing a timeless masterpiece which portrayed something fundamental about the human condition—all of which she said to Geoff as they had a nightcap in a bar near his apartment. "It was a tragedy, yet I never laughed so hard in my life. How can that be?"

"Arthur Miller is a genius, that's why. Faced with great emotion, a human being, in a theater, at least, can find an outlet in either tears or laughter. Miller chose to give the audience a chance to laugh." He smiled. "It was either that or supply hankies to everyone."

"Yes." Her eyes were still bright from remembrance of the play. "I'm glad you told me the line Biff rendered offstage. I didn't know what everyone was laughing at."

"I figured you might need a little help there."

"It was very funny."

He looked at her a long moment, then took her hand across the table. "I've never seen you more beautiful. Your eyes are so bright. They look like star sapphires."

"Wow!" She smiled. "All that—and after all these months of living together." She squeezed his fingers. "I had a good time, Geoff. Thank you."

His expression turned serious. "Make you like New York any better?"

She saw the change in his mood, mirrored it. "You know I like New York, Geoff. It's—"

"But not all the time."

She sighed. "I miss Westport, and I do look forward to weekends." Now she gave a wan smile. "I'm just a country bumpkin, I guess. But that doesn't mean I don't like the city—like being with you. It's just—"

"You want a nest."

She stared at him. "You understand that?"

"Yes. Nest building is a female trait. Comes with the genes." Now he smiled. "I'm not sure men don't have it too. At least they want to know their woman is safe somewhere, protected, while they're out killing mastodons."

"And washing his socks while he's gone." She laughed.

"Did cavemen wear socks?" He joined her laughter a moment, then abruptly turned serious. "Have you given any thought to that question I asked you awhile back?"

"Marriage? All the time, Geoff. I do love you."

"But you're not entirely happy."

She sighed. "It has nothing to do with you, Geoff. You're being wonderful, all I could want, and that heavenly machine is—"

"Yes, isn't it. I know it makes me far more relaxed about you. Have you noticed that?"

"Oh, yes." She smiled. "I notice everything about you."

"I know. I can't get away with a thing." His quick laugh faded. "I've been thinking, Irish. Kevin O'Neill, the actor, not only makes me a nice piece of change, he's taken root and proliferated. He made several referrals and my client list is getting so long I may have to take in a partner."

She smiled. "I'm not at all surprised. You're very good. Look at the money you've saved me."

"Yeah. Pretty soon you'll be richer than me. The point I'm getting at is that I've been thinking of investing in some real estate. I was thinking of a place out in the country, a little land, not a lot, maybe a couple of acres." He grinned. "I haven't mowed lawn in years. Then I'd like to take a stab at gardening. Used to do it when I was a kid. A few fresh vegetables would be nice, wouldn't they?"

Irish held her breath. She knew where this was leading.

"The house? Nothing pretentious, maybe colonial or saltbox, perhaps something older with lots of character. I'd want trees around it. Wouldn't have to be large, but enough rooms to spread out in, raise a family. How's it sound to you?"

"Heavenly." She was grinning radiantly, couldn't help it. "Who'd you have in mind to share it with?"

"I already popped the question, remember? Would a house in the country help you make up your mind?"

"Oh, yes!" Then a thought came to her, dampening her enthusiasm. "But you don't like to commute."

"I know. I wasn't thinking necessarily of Westport. Maybe some place closer in—Noroton Heights or Cos Cob, possibly Greenwich. Unless you're wedded to Connecticut—"

"I'm not."

"—it could be Harrison, Port Chester, maybe White Plains in New York State."

"That wouldn't matter."

"It would be a shorter commute. Then I thought I'd outfit an office at home, work there a couple of days a week. I might even pick up a few clients in the area."

"Oh, Geoff, it sounds wonderful!"

"If it isn't too big a financial squeeze, I thought I'd keep my place on 73rd Street. We could use it for nights in the city—or I could rent it out."

"Yes."

"As for your beach cottage, maybe you could try to buy it. I'm not sure we can get a place on the water. It might be nice to have the cottage for—"

"Yes, yes."

He grinned at her. "Yes to what? Yes to owning real estate or yes to marriage?"

"Both."

He shook his head. "No. I don't want that."

She was surprised. "Really? I thought all this was—"

"I mean I don't want you to say yes right now. I want you to think about it, about me, about what our life together would be like. I want kids, Irish, good kids. I want them to grow up in a nice environment with fresh air, lots of room to play, good schools—the kind of life I had."

She felt filled to overflowing with happiness. "I love you, Geoff Winter."

"I want you to be sure, Irish—absolutely sure."

"I am."

He shook his head. "Take a couple of days, ruminate over everything. Then if the answer is still yes, we'll take a few days and start looking for a house." He smiled. "I can't wait to get going on a family."

She laughed. "It does take some time, you know."

"Sure. That's why we have to get started."

Her reply was a knowing smile, eyes bright with anticipation.

She stood up, and he dropped money on top of the check. They left the bar, walking hand in hand the block and a half to his apartment house. It was a cold night and she wore no gloves, yet her hand within his was warm. They were alone in the elevator still holding hands. Gently, his thumb caressed the back of her hand, rolling over her knuckles, sliding sensuously between her fingers. No words were uttered, but their eyes met. Irish couldn't miss noticing the desire and eagerness that brightened Geoff's eyes. She loved the way he looked right before they made love.

Without releasing her hand, he unlocked the door and they entered. He closed the door then with his free hand, accepted Sam's greeting, and sent him to lie down. No lights were turned on, yet they could see because the drapes were open and the room was lit with the lights of the city, a fairyland extending into the distance.

They had made love many times during the month of their togetherness. Many were memorable to Irish. She knew instinctively that although she'd only ever had one other man, Geoff Winter was truly special. He brought inventiveness and imagination to his lovemaking so that nothing was ever quite the same. It was as though he refused to allow familiarity to dull their passion even the littlest bit. He made her feel he was somehow *privileged* to love her.

They threw their coats carelessly on a chair and he pulled her against him. Leaning forward, he kissed her oh so slowly and thoroughly.

She shivered with desire as with one hand he massaged the back of her neck and with the other unbuttoned her blouse. She felt the heat within her building. Impatiently she helped him undress her, and then began pulling his clothes off him. When they had finished discarding the hindrances to their pleasure, she stood before him, mere inches away, and saw his eyes fill once again with awe, delight and appreciation. *May that never go away,* she thought.

His hands came to her waist, then moved upward roaming over her breasts, her back, her neck, shooting a current of sharp desire to every part of her body. She had to close her eyes, unable to keep them open as sensations streaked through her. His hands, cool and smooth, molded her shoulders and arms, then returned to her back going downward, squeezing her buttocks, inching down to tease the backs of her thighs. She quivered with anticipation. For all the roaming of his hands, he had failed to caress her where she most wanted to feel his touch. Being deprived, she became more eager and expectant.

She kissed him hungrily, giving him everything in that kiss, thrusting her tongue against his, running her hands wildly over his muscular back and shoulders.

When at last his hand found what ached her the most, she felt her whole body sigh. But only for a moment as pleasures swirled through her, dizzying her, taking her breath away. In a moment she forced her eyes open, saw him; his eyes were closed and she understood. He was trying to join her in her wholly tactile experience. Her hands moved lower, grasping and fondling his buttocks, then slid around to the tops of his thighs. She saw his eyes squint, felt him jerk and tremble. Her hands moved again and again and again. . . . His mouth came open, his breath shortened, and his hands upon her became temporarily still. He groaned with satisfaction. She was thrilled that she was pleasuring him so profoundly.

A little later when the bed was beneath them, Irish felt for the first time that she truly gave herself to him. Never before had she understood him, his needs not just for release, but for imagination, daring, boldness, and especially for sharing—that underpinning of love.

And when at last she welcomed him she knew that her blessed filling was his deepest fulfillment. In the culmination of their rhythmic movements, her back arched, and she cried out in ecstasy shuddering helplessly as the ultimate pleasure overwhelmed her. At that moment she had such a sense of *him*, not just his power, his straining, the physical manifestation of his release, but what making love truly meant to him.

For the first time in their relationship she did not release him. Hers was the power now. And she saw the wonder, truly amazement in his eyes, as she aroused him again and began to truly plumb the depths of him, of each other.

Irish had never before felt so deeply in love with Geoff or so close in body or spirit to him as she did that night. She regretted being on the Pill for she knew she would have conceived. That would have made it perfection.

At midmorning Sam summoned her to the teletype. KAREN HERE. CAN'T HAVE LUNCH. TONS OF WORK. SORRY.

Irish typed back: THAT'S OK. COULD WE MEET FOR COCKTAILS LATER? GOT SOMETHING IMPORTANT TO TALK TO YOU ABOUT.

There was a delay, then these words: SURE. LOVE TO. WHERE?

FOUR SEASONS, FIVE-THIRTYISH.

THAT'S POSH.

IT'S SPECIAL. I'M BUYING. SEE YOU. BYE.

Irish watched Karen's BYE appear on the paper. Silly of her to want to tell Karen she and Geoff were going to get married. Then she smiled. No, it wasn't. Such good news should be shared. And she'd want Karen to be her maid of honor. Doris could be matron of honor. Where would they have the wedding? Westport? Or should they go out to Ohio where his family was? It was something to talk to Geoff about. They had lots of plans to make.

Karen was there ahead of her, sitting at one of the tables to the rear, away from the bar where it was quiet. Irish stood over her a moment, looking down, smiling.

"You look absolutely radiant. What're you up to?"

Irish saw her quizzical look. "Geoff's meeting us here in a bit. We'll stick him with the tab." She slid into a seat opposite Karen.

"Who cares about tabs? I asked what you're up to."

Irish had planned to tease her, insist there was nothing, drag out the announcement. Now she knew she couldn't. "Geoff and I are going to be married."

Karen's reaction surprised her. Her face became lit with a truly beatific smile and her eyes filled with tears. "I'm so happy for you—for you both."

"Are you surprised?"

Karen seemed to shuck off her emotion. "Are you kidding? You two have been obvious from the start. When did he ask you?"

"Sometime ago, actually. I'm awful, I guess, keeping him waiting for an answer. But I wanted to be sure."

"And now you've said yes."

Irish shook her head. "Not quite. We talked about it last night. I would have said yes then, but he wanted me to think about it." Her radiant smile came again. "He's meeting us here. I'm saying yes whether he wants to hear it or not."

Karen laughed. "I'm sure he does. What made up your mind?"

Irish told her about their plans to buy a house in the country. "That did it. Living in two places, neither one really home, bothered me. This way—"

"You have the best of both worlds. I'm so happy for you, Irish."

"Me, too." The waiter came. She ordered Chablis. "You've been married twice. Would you give me some advice?"

A generous laugh cascaded from Karen. "Me? That's the blind leading the halt, isn't it?"

"Do you think it will work with Geoff and me?"

"I don't see why not. I've never seen two people so much in love."

"But love isn't enough. Every couple starts out in love. What happens to it? Where does it go? I'm serious, Karen. I want to avoid—"

"My mistakes?"

"I didn't mean that."

"You should. Nobody gives me as a reference for connubial bliss. To answer your question, I think marriages fail because people never solved their problems before marriage. They just hoped love would solve everything and it doesn't."

"Do you think Geoff and I have solved all our problems?"

"How would I know, Irish? Only you can answer that. I only know there was one big one."

"My deafness? You know about our problem with that?"

"I'm not altogether dumb, Irish. It was obvious at first. He was treating you like glass. But I don't see it much anymore."

"He's much better. Just took some adjustment and getting used to. Actually the teletype solved most of it." She looked down, running her finger around the rim of her wineglass. "There's only one thing. Sometimes I wonder why he wants a deaf girl."

Karen laughed. "That's easy. Just look in the mirror. All I can tell you for certain is the man is wild about you. I've been with him for six years, and I can tell you one thing. He's a man who's found the one he's been looking for."

Irish smiled. "That's nice. And you're right. Why don't you tell me I'm being silly."

"You're being silly. Have you set the date?"

"No, we really haven't discussed the wedding. All I know is I want you to be my maid of honor. Will you?"

Another laugh escaped Karen. "I'm not sure I qualify as a maid anymore, but, yes. I'm honored—and so lucky to have you for a friend."

"Look who's talking."

When Geoff came Karen stood up and hugged him, kissing his cheek. "I hear you're about to get good news. I'm so happy for you both."

Irish couldn't read Geoff's expression.

"Fine thing. A guy asks a girl to marry him and gets his answer from his secretary."

Karen reacted. "Did I let the cat out of the bag?"

"Hardly." He bent to kiss Irish. "Then it's yes?"

"Yes, and yes again, forever yes." She raised her lips to his.

"Stop it, you two. We're in a public place and there are laws that prohibit that kind of behavior."

Geoff sat down next to Irish and motioned to the waiter. When he came, he ordered champagne. "Got to celebrate, don't you think?"

"Not me. Just you two. I don't like being a crowd."

Geoff wouldn't hear of Karen's leaving. "Been busy today." He reached in his right-hand coat pocket. "Might as well see this now, Karen. Irish'll just be down at the office tomorrow, showing you. You'll never get any work done."

He handed the box to Irish and she accepted, eyes bright, luminous with expectancy. Slowly she opened it, blinked. "Oh, Geoff!" It was the biggest diamond she had ever seen, dazzling, blue-white, at least four karats. Wide-eyed, speechless, she could only turn the box, show it to Karen. The oval stone caught the light as she moved it.

"My word! Geoff, it's *huge!*"

"Had a hard time finding it. Here." He removed the stone from the box. "I'm supposed to put it on, I think."

Irish extended a slender finger on her left hand, felt the ring slip on as though it had become part of her life. She looked at it, scintillating on her finger, bright as a beacon, then at the smiling face of her intended. She was near tears as she threw her arms around him, hugging him tightly, her wet cheek against his. But the diamond beckoned. She moved her hand, saw it over his shoulder. "It's so beautiful. I never. . . . It must've cost a fortune."

He held her away so he could speak. "We may have to get a smaller house at that." Then he laughed. "Speaking of that, I also busied myself talking to real estate agents today."

Karen said, "Sounds to me like you were awfully sure she was going to say yes."

Irish said, "I think he suspected it."

"It seems there is no shortage of homes for sale. The realtor is lining them up. We're to spend all day Saturday looking at properties."

Public place or no public place, Irish kissed him. Then for the next few minutes both told Karen about their ideas for their new life. Finally Karen announced she really did have to get home and she gathered up her purse to leave.

Her eyes mischievous, Irish asked, "By the way how are you and Jay Selkirk getting along?"

"Know what? I detest matchmakers. That was a dirty trick, Irish, inviting *me* to lunch the other day then sneaking him in."

Irish laughed. "I didn't tell you to go out with him. I merely introduced a couple of my friends."

"It was still a dirty trick."

"Why?"

"Because he's so damned nice."

Geoff piped in. "I wondered why you've been humming in the office lately."

Karen was standing now. "You noticed that, did you?"

"I don't want to lose a good secretary."

"You won't."

Irish laughed. "I'm not too sure. Jay can be persistent."

"You might be right," Karen said. "There are no sparks. The earth doesn't move. It just becomes a very comfortable, most inhabitable place. And speaking of the devil, I better run. We've a date."

Geoff watched Karen leave, then turned to Irish. She had that wondrous feeling of intimacy, just the two of them in the whole world.

"Happy?"

"No, miserable."

"Me, too."

He kissed her, lightly, almost formally, yet she felt the sharp stab of sensation at her lips. "Will that go away when we're married?"

"Not a chance. With you and me it's a permanent affliction. You're just going to have to live with it."

"I'll try." She leaned against him, feeling the heat of him. What she really wanted to do was go home, be alone with him.

"I had some more good news today."

"I don't think I can stand anymore for one day."

"I think you'll like this. I talked by phone with some people Judge Burroughs put me on to. It seems we might be in luck. There's a girl seven, a boy nine, brother and sister. These people think we might be the right placement for them."

Irish shook her head. "What're you talking about?"

"Be sort of nice, wouldn't it? Kind of an instant family—boy and girl. Course I haven't seen them. They may not be right. But I think they're worth checking out."

Again she shook her head, then she moved away from him, as though distance would alleviate her bewilderment. "I don't understand. Are you talking about adoption?"

"Sure." He smiled. "Happens all the time."

"But why?"

"You know why. We can't have kids—and I'd like at least a couple. We talked about it last night."

"Not about adoption. Is there something wrong with you? Have you had a vasectomy?"

"Me? I'm fine. But you know *you* can't."

She stared at him wide-eyed, then swallowed hard as understanding came to her. She looked around, saw the other people, then looked back at him. She was dismayed, felt she couldn't breathe. Then her anger slammed into her. Visibly shaking, she stood up.

"Where're you going?"

"We'd better go home, Geoff—and talk! Right now!"

She entered the apartment, dropped her coat on a chair, and went to the window of the living room, staring out at the lighted city around her. In the cab from the Four Seasons, her anger had given way to the deep dejection she now felt. She felt deeply wounded, right to the core of herself.

Her back was to him. She sensed he was talking to her, but she didn't really care about what he was saying. Slowly she turned to face him.

"What's the matter with you, Irish? What have I done now?"

That didn't help. He was treating her like a petulant child who was throwing a tantrum. Did she really know this man? "Why do you want to adopt children?"

"You know why. The one thing we can't do is have kids."

She saw the earnestness in his eyes. He really believed what he said, and that knowledge only deepened her wound. It wasn't possible, not after all this time. She exhaled a sharp sigh. She had a sense of being on some kind of terrible slide to oblivion as she said, "Geoff, I'm just as capable of having children as the next woman."

"You're not, Irish, and you know it."

She stared at him, shaking her head in disbelief. She had a feeling all these words had been written long ago, chiseled in granite, foreordained to be uttered at this time. And she was helpless against them. "You don't think my deafness is hereditary, do you? It isn't. I went deaf from spinal meningitis. My children will hear just fine."

"I know that. But you still won't be able to raise them."

She'd known that was what he meant back at the Four Seasons. She had even known he was going to utter those exact words. Yet, hearing him actually say them hurt her terribly. They savaged her as a person and as a woman, and the pain brought tears to her eyes. She could not hear the choke in her voice as she said, "How can you think such a thing?"

"Look, Irish, I know how well you get along. You're marvelous, truly amazing. I love you for it, but—"

"Don't patronize me, Geoff."

"I'm not, believe me, I'm not, but there are certain things you have to face. You have to learn to accept your own limitations. You can do most everything, but one thing you can't is raise children. If you think about it, you'll know that is true. I *have* thought about it—a lot. You won't hear a baby cry when he's hungry, wet, needs you, or is in danger. Don't you see how impossible that'll be? It's too big a risk to take. You can't want to and if you do, I won't let you."

She watched his moving lips form the words that were so hateful to her. And she knew what they foretold. She felt she was already entering a dark painful void.

"A child learns to speak by hearing adults, mimicking them. You must know that, Irish. Think about it, as I have. I know you can speak, but you won't hear the children's voices, correct their speech. I don't want my kids growing up talking funny. Neither do you. The solution is to adopt children who already know how to talk. Maybe this brother and sister will be right for us. If not, we'll—"

She closed her eyes to blot out words she didn't want to know. They were too obscene. Then she felt his hands on her shoulders and opened her eyes.

"I know I'm right, honey."

She shook her head. "You don't know what you're talking about."

150

"Irish, I love you. I'll do anything I can to make you happy. I'll even move up to Connecticut and commute. But on this issue I know I'm right. I have to do what is right for both of us—no matter how much it hurts you."

"You're wrong, Geoff, terribly wrong."

"I am not! I've thought about it. I've talked to people."

"You've talked to others—about me, about us?" She felt an incipient surge of anger. "Thanks a lot!"

"Don't be this way, *please.* I'm not wrong."

"Oh, but you are. Deaf people raise hearing children all the time."

"Not my kids!"

There it was, the final, fatal wound, striking deep, to seal the end of their affair just when she'd thought it was blossoming into a lifetime commitment. She turned, stalked into the bedroom, lifted her suitcase from the closet to the bed, intending to pack.

He had followed. "Where are you going?"

"Home, back to Westport where I belong."

"But why?" He seemed genuinely puzzled.

"To pick up the pieces of my life, try to put them back together."

"Dammit, Irish, don't be this way. You know I don't want to hurt you, but we have to face certain facts and deal with them. I'm trying to. All you're doing is running away. I thought you were tougher than that."

He was not only insulting her as a woman, he was now engaging in character assassination. Her eyes narrowed, glinting a little like blue steel. "You're right about facing facts, Geoff. Only we're facing different ones. The fact I have to deal with is your deep-seated prejudice about me. You simply can't get over it."

"Not that again! We're talking about having kids."

"This has nothing to do with children. It's about you, your attitude toward me. You just can't accept me as a reasonably normal person who has had to adjust to an impairment—and not that an uncommon one at that. Lots of people are hard of hearing or deaf. But you can't live with that." She shook her head. "I guess you can't help yourself. To you I'm handicapped—a cripple. I'm marked in your mind for special handling—fragile, do not drop, do not permit to have children. In your mind I'm in a wheelchair. I need a blanket to sit on." Her anger was a full flood now.

"That's not fair!"

"You're right—only you're the one who's not fair. You can't accept me as I am—and I can't live with someone who sees me as a cripple." Suddenly she saw his engagement ring on her finger. She twisted it off. "You can get your money back on this, I'm sure." She laid it on the nightstand.

"I love you, Irish. Don't be this way."

She went to the closet, jerking out a handful of hangered garments. He was there when she turned around.

"I thought we had all this special treatment thing settled."

"I did, too. Apparently I was wrong."

"Irish, dammit, I don't think of you as a cripple."

"Don't you? You just said it. *Not my kids!* Those were your very words. *Not my kids!* You don't want your kids raised by a deaf person. You don't want them *contaminated!*"

"Dammit, Irish, I—"

"Fine with me. I'm going to have children and you better believe they aren't going to be yours. I wouldn't want them near you."

He shook with rage. She had hurt him terribly, but his words belied it. "I'm not going to fight with you, Irish. I love you."

"I wonder. Do you love *me*—or your martyrdom? Wonderful Geoff Winter. He's so devoted to that crippled girl. She's deaf, you know. Couldn't get along without him. Poor Geoff Winter. She couldn't even give him children."

She saw his face was red with anger. "I don't care what you say or do, Irish. I know I'm right and I'm doing what's best for us."

NINE

The crowd gasped as one, utterly shocked as the sculpture of Venus was unveiled. It was an outrage and some faces were already turning to anger at the woman who had modeled for the statue. Through it all Cleopatra stood proudly, regally, her left hand holding that of her young son, her eyes fixed on Julius Caesar, father of her child, the ruler of Rome.

Irish stepped back and tried to get the effect of the painting. She had hoped to portray the essence of Cleopatra. She had a pronounced Semitic nose and wasn't beautiful by modern standards. Indeed beauty alone would not have captured Caesar and Marc Antony, both Roman leaders. She had to have had something more, and Irish tried to portray her intelligence, pride, fiery independence as a queen in her own right, then overlay that with an innate sensuousness. The statue being naked surely helped.

She looked down at Sam, sitting at her feet. "What d'you think, love? Would you go for her, give up your empire just to be with her?" She laughed. "If she gave you enough doggie biscuits, you probably would."

Irish decided she was pleased with the painting. A lot of study and discussion had gone into the decision to portray this scene. It was decided first that Cleopatra's affair with Marc Antony was sort of disreputable. Go with Julius Caesar. For a time everybody at the ad agency and oil company wanted to do the famous scene in which Cleopatra emerged from the rug in which she was smuggled before the conquering Roman. Irish had finally convinced them to use this moment when the statue of Venus was unveiled. It had shocked all of Rome. He had used his paramour, an Egyptian at that, as model for a Roman goddess. It led directly to his murder by Brutus.

"Yes, Sam, I like it. Very sexy, very titillating. Why not? All the women rulers don't have to be stony-faced curmudgeons. Wait till I do Catherine the Great. She slept with the world. And Queen Anne of England had seventeen pregnancies. She and the king must have been doing something besides issuing royal edicts."

At once a mental image of Geoff flitted across her mind. She shook her head. "Can't think about that, Sam. It's a no-no. Want a run?"

The late March day was cool, blustery, Compo Beach deserted, but when she returned to her cottage she had worked up a good sweat, which pleased her. She stood in the kitchen now, drinking orange juice, trying to think positively about her life.

She was doing pretty well, better than she had ever figured she would. Work was her salvation. She had clung to it as a life raft, discovering she could concentrate and draw well. Thereafter she used it to keep away the ghosts and goblins which rattled the bars of her mind. What was the psychological term? Oh, yes, sublimation.

In the beginning she had told herself Geoff Winter had died. She loved him, she always would, but he was gone from her life, buried in a vault in a

155

graveyard somewhere. No point in thinking about him, dwelling on the what-might-have-beens. Get on with her life, start a new one. What a wonderful opportunity! Doesn't everyone like to begin a new life?

He hadn't made it at all easy for her. She glanced at the coffee table in the main room. On it was an immense bouquet of red roses. He had started with a single rose on the day after she left, then increased the gift exponentially, one each day until this morning she had received a box of thirty-seven roses. She had never calculated how many roses he had sent, but it had to be many dozens. Some had died, but she was still left with a huge bouquet. Each day the note was the same: I LOVE YOU, IRISH. I WON'T LOSE YOU. She sighed. Her first impulse had been to throw the flowers out. But they were beautiful and her sense of thrift prevented that. Give them away? No. That would be proof she was wrong in leaving him. That's what he believed, what he wanted her to think. Not so. She made the roses a symbol of the correctness of her decision. They supported her certainty that marriage to Geoff Winter simply would never have worked.

Her anger at him had long since dissolved, replaced by an elemental sadness. She felt dead inside, numb. There was a great big hollow place inside her which nothing would fill. Yet she ate and slept, smiled and laughed, talked to people—and worked, well and hard. She got her exercise. Life indeed did go on. Something was missing. Too bad. Just a matter of finding a substitute. Geoff Winter was gone, dead. Psychologists called it extinction. Yes, she would render Geoff Winter extinct.

Her biggest problem was that she had changed. She was more sophisticated, more sure of herself.

Self-doubt, dependency, desire for approval from others were largely gone, along with the presentiment that there was more to life than work and friends. There wasn't. Well, at least not for her.

Sam did his doorbell number, jumping up and racing for the door. Irish followed and opened it on Bill Clark. She really wasn't glad to see him, but her smile as she let him in belied that.

"Chilly day out there. Think we'll ever get spring?"

"We did, last Tuesday—at least that's what the calendar declared."

She really didn't want him to stay, but he was already unzipping his ski jacket and there was nothing to do but accept him. "Do you want some coffee —a drink perhaps?"

"Coffee would be nice—if you have it."

"Instant all right?"

"Sure."

Glad to be away from him, she went to the kitchen, turned on the gas under the teakettle, and busied herself bringing out mugs. Bill Clark was a mistake, one she deeply regretted. She had met him at Staples High School, here in Westport, where he was a guidance counselor. She had gone to apply for a job as art teacher in the night adult ed classes. Thought more activity might be good for her. No opening. She came away with Bill Clark.

It had been a deliberate act on her part. One way to rid herself of Geoff Winter, she decided, was to become involved with another man. Bill Clark was pleasant, friendly, easygoing, sort of tweedy. She thought he might be comfortable. Probably his brown hair, freckles, and Charlie Brown look—he reminded her of Derek Parkins—had something to do with it. They had gone out to dinner, then a movie. She hadn't told him she was deaf and as far as she knew he hadn't realized it. They got along. He told a lot of stories about the drug and behavioral problems among teenagers in this posh ex-urban community. Surprising, really. Money wasn't everything.

He was there in the kitchen. "Hope you don't mind my dropping in?"

"No, it's all right."

"Irish—" He hesitated, as though uncertain of his next words. "I've missed you the past week."

She tried to smile. "I'm sorry. Been awfully busy." She made a gesture toward her work area. He went to look at her easel and she was glad to have him go.

It had been a terrible thing for her to do. On the second date she had made a conscious decision to go to bed with him. Sex with another man would surely exorcise Geoff from her body, if not her mind. She had dressed seductively, even convinced herself that Bill Clark was highly attractive and she wanted him badly. It hadn't worked. After a few kisses the heavy breathing was all on his part. She knew she had turned him on, but she was dead inside, filled with loathing for herself. She had gotten out of it, but not at all gracefully.

She brought the coffee cups, and they spoke a minute about her Cleopatra painting.

"I want to see you, Irish. I know I was too fast the other night, but—"

"It wasn't you, Bill. It was me. I thought I wanted it, but I was wrong."

"I think you did. In fact, I know it. You just need more time." He smiled. "It's TGIF. Let's go out to dinner, enjoy ourselves."

She motioned with her hand toward her drawing board. "I'm sorry. I can't tonight."

"It's Friday, Irish—time to relax, have fun."

She hated this. "No, not tonight."

"Have you other plans?"

"No, I just—" She saw hurt rise in his eyes and wished she'd lied.

"Is it something I've done—the other night?"

"No, I—" She stopped thinking of excuses, being on the defensive. The only fair thing was to tell him how she felt. "Bill, I don't think we ought to see each other anymore."

"But why?"

Suddenly she realized she'd never done this before. Almost thirty years old and this was a first. She didn't know how to do it. "I can't, that's all."

"Is there something wrong with me?"

"Oh, no, please don't think that. You're a very . . . nice person. It's just—" She sighed. "It's me. Nothing will ever come of it. You're better off with—"

"I only asked you to dinner, Irish."

"I know, but—*please.*" She felt trapped, confused, ensnared in a situation she hated. "Would you mind going now?" She brought him his coat.

"I'm not dumb, Irish." He motioned toward the coffee table. "All those roses. You're on the rebound."

She tried to hold his jacket for him, but he snatched it from her and donned it himself, leaving her to endure the angry hurt in his eyes. When he reached the door she said, "I'm sorry, Bill. You don't deserve this."

"I'm the one who's sorry—for you. Whoever he was, he isn't worth it."

"Yes, he was."

When he was gone Irish was left feeling rotten. She railed at herself. There had to have been a better way. Why was she such a numbskull? What possessed her to get involved with him? Never again.

Agitated, her peace of mind gone, the walls of the cottage closing in, she took Sam in the car and drove around awhile, finally ending up in the kitchen of Doris Parkins.

"You look like you need a shoulder to cry on."

"I suppose."

"I wondered when it would happen. You've toughed it out for over a month."

Irish sighed. "It's not what you think. It's not Geoff—somebody else, a guy I met. We went out a couple of times. I even played the big seduction scene with him—then couldn't go through with it. He came over just now. I told him I didn't want to see him again. It was awful."

"It usually is."

"He's a nice man. He did nothing to deserve it, yet I managed to hurt him. First time I ever realized the position of the male. He's supposed to be the aggressor. Every time he approaches a woman he puts his ego on the line. When she rejects him—and for no reason other than maybe sparks don't fly— he's hurt."

Doris smiled. "I imagine he'll get over it."

"No wonder men—really nice men, I mean—quit trying. Doris, do you realize that was the first time I ever did that to a man?"

"No, it wasn't. I can think of one in New York right now who is quite miserable. And wasn't there one before that? You're a regular femme fatale."

Irish gaped at her. "They were different!"

160

"How? Only in that they gave you good excuses so you wouldn't feel guilty?"

Her anger flared. "I'm not guilty about Geoff."

"Aren't you?"

"He's the one who said 'not my kids!' He's the one who thinks I'm some kind of leper who'll—"

"So he said something stupid. Every man does. You should hear Derek. I spent the first year of my marriage in tears until I learned to fight back."

"I can fight, Doris."

She laughed. "Oh, I believe that. How about a cup of tea? I'm supposed to be a shoulder, remember?"

Irish watched her friend put the pot on. "Would you make a phone call for me—to New York?"

"Of course. Who do you want to call?"

"Her name's Karen Chambers. She's a . . . a friend. Just ask her if she could come out and spend the weekend with me?"

She gave Doris the number of Geoff's office, then watched, reading lips as Doris spoke. "Hi, my name is Doris Parkins. I'm a friend of Irish O'Brien here in Westport." Pause. "Oh, she's fine. Sitting here in my kitchen right now. She asked me to call and see if you can come out and spend the weekend with her." Pause, then Doris turned to her. "She says she'd love to. Can she bring Ricky?"

"Oh, yes, please. Tell her to come tonight."

Irish saw that message repeated, then Doris turned back to her. "She wants directions. Never mind, I'll give them to her." That was done, the phone hung up, then Doris said, "You'll have company about eight-thirty or nine."

"Wonderful! Thank you."

"Who, may I ask, is Karen Chambers who provokes all this happiness?"

161

Irish hesitated. "If you must know, she's Geoff's secretary."

"Aha! Now it comes out. There's more than one way to skin a cat."

"It's not what you think. We became good friends. I miss her."

"Sur-r-r-re, tell me about it."

"It's true. This has nothing to do with Geoff. It's all over between us."

"No, it's not. You're just on hiatus, like the summer reruns on television. If ever I've seen a girl in love and miserable, it's you. One of these days you're going to quit trying to tough it out and do what you have to."

"You're awful, Doris. You think you know everything. You don't."

"Don't I? Are you going to deny you're in love with Geoff and miserable?"

"As a matter of fact, I'm not. I don't need you to tell me that. What you don't know is that there's not a blessed thing to be done about it—except get over it, which I'm doing."

"You're doing a lousy job, if you ask me."

"Who asked?"

Doris laughed. "My, but you're fun to fight with." She served the tea. "Lemon?"

"Please."

That was brought from the refrigerator. "May I tell you something?"

"You will anyway—even if I don't like being on the defensive this way."

"Can't make you feel any worse than you do already. Listen, honey, I know he's awful. But all men are—some of the time anyway."

"You don't know, Doris."

"I think I do. He said 'not my kids!' Which means

162

he considers you an unfit mother. He wants kids and you aren't good enough. That about it?"

Irish sighed. "Something like that."

"Then show him how wrong he is."

"How? Go out and have a couple of kids and—"

"I don't know. But it seems to me there ought to be some way to wise up the dumb sap."

Irish shook her head. "Nice try, but there isn't any way. Geoff sees me as a poor little deaf girl— and I can't live with that. It's hopeless."

Doris shrugged. "So be it. Drink your tea."

Their hug was prolonged and Irish's eyes filled with tears. She hadn't realized until that moment just how fond she was of Karen Chambers. Then she greeted her son, Ricky Davenport. He was tall for his age, serious, and just about the handsomest boy Irish had ever seen. He had his mother's light brown hair, a squarish face, wide firm mouth, and gorgeous blue-violet eyes.

"I was to ask if I may call you Irish."

"Please do."

"You're very beautiful."

Irish laughed. "From someone who lives with your Mom, that's high praise. Thank you."

His eyes seemed to probe into her. "Mom says you're deaf and I should face you when I talk."

Irish glanced at Karen.

"I felt he ought to know. Do you mind?"

"No." She looked at Ricky. "Yes, I'm deaf."

"You can't hear me?"

"I know what you're saying, so it seems as though I hear you. But, really, I can't hear a thing."

"What's it like to be deaf?"

Irish could think of a thousand answers, but she said only, "Quiet." She smiled.

163

"You really know what I'm saying? You read my lips?"

Irish saw his enthusiasm. The directness of children! With most people she wouldn't have wanted these questions, but this was all right. "I think so."

"Supercalifragilisticexpialidocious."

"That's too easy." She laughed. "I know the word. Try something I don't."

The boy pondered a moment. "Frimlizzy, muckytoddle."

"Hmm. Frimlizzy, muckytoddle."

He grinned. "Hey, that's great. Can I learn to do that?"

"Sure. Just turn off the sound on the TV and have a go."

They hadn't eaten and Irish served a late supper, then did her best to satisfy Ricky's curiosity about her work. He asked a million questions and seemed in awe that his mother knew, and now he knew, someone who had actually drawn things he'd seen. "Wait till I tell the kids. They won't believe it."

Irish asked if she could keep him. "He's good for the ego."

Finally, after the eleven o'clock news and a bit of Johnny Carson, Ricky settled down on the couch and fell asleep. She and Karen had a chance to talk quietly in the kitchen.

"He's a wonderful boy. No wonder you love him."

"He's my whole life."

"No Jay?"

The beautiful secretary raised already arched eyebrows. "Yes, there's still a Jay. But we're taking it slow. Both of us have made mistakes. We don't want to again."

"Prognosis? Are you in love?"

"I think so. He more than me."

"Is that a problem?"

"No. He seems satisfied with my . . . my performance."

"Is that all it is—a performance?"

"Don't misunderstand. I don't fake. I like it. I like him. It's just not—"

"You told me. The earth still spins on its axis. Have you talked to him about that?"

"As a matter of fact, yes. You now how it is. Divorced people early on reveal the nitty-gritty of their former marriages—at least Jay and I did. It's one of the things I like best about him. We can talk."

"No fisticuffs?"

"None, thank God. I think he accepts me the way I am. It is enough for him."

Irish felt a twinge of regret deep within, but said, "Sounds like you're doing fine."

"And you? Or don't you want to talk about it?"

Irish sighed. "It's okay. You can't come all the way out here and not wonder. I'm doing all right, Karen. My work hasn't suffered. It's going great guns, in fact. As for the rest. . . ." A shrug was her answer.

"I see you keep the roses he sends. I figured you'd throw them out."

Irish explained why she didn't. "I do get rid of the cards. They're all the same."

"Lonely?"

"I suppose. I just don't think about it—except today." She told her about Bill Clark. "That's why I had Doris phone you and ask you to come out. I'm glad you're here."

"So am I. I've wanted to see you. That silent teleprinter is a constant reminder of you."

"He still has it?"

"Oh, yes. Nothing has changed really. He never says anything, but I feel he believes he hasn't lost you. You're just away temporarily."

"Well, he has lost me. It's for the best—for both of us."

"I didn't tell him I was coming here."

"I figured you wouldn't." Irish bit at her lip. "I might as well ask and get it over with. How is he?"

"About like you. Amazingly so in fact. He's a bear for work. I can hardly keep up with him. And he's not very happy. Something important is missing from his life." Karen paused. "He's still in love with you. Are you with him?"

"Of course. How long has it been? A little over a month? Love doesn't go away that quickly."

"If ever. What went wrong, Irish? When I last saw you two together, he had just given you that beautiful diamond. You both were so happy, so in love."

The memories were real pain for Irish. "I know. It surprised me, too." She told her in detail what had happened, even relating much of the language of their quarrel. "My friend Doris told me today I'm wrong. Is that what you're going to do?"

"Not me. He sounds like a pigheaded sap to me." She smiled and reached out, stroking Irish's hair. "Even I know deaf parents raise hearing children. I don't know how they do it, but I know they do. Isn't there something you can do to educate him?"

"Like what?"

"I don't know. Maybe you could send him an article on the subject—or a book. Make him understand how wrong he is."

"That's not the problem, Karen. You ought to know that. You just said Jay accepts you as you are. That's all I want—acceptance of me, warts and all, deaf or hearing, blind, lame, stupid, or whatever.

I'm not special and I don't want to be treated special. I want to be just me—and loved for that."

"I understand, Irish."

"And it's something I'm never going to get from Geoff. He's a wonderful man. I do love him. But he has one flaw. Try as he will, he just can't accept me as a reasonably normal person. It's been a problem all the way along."

"A fatal flaw."

Irish saw her nodding her head in understanding. "I tried to ignore it. I hoped it would go away. And that was a mistake—leading to unhappiness for us both."

"Better now than after marriage."

Irish nodded. "Am I right?"

"You've convinced me."

Saturday morning dawned sunny and warmer, leading to a truly fun weekend. Ricky loved the beach and found a friend in Sam. Karen lamented. "I guess I'm going to have to get him a dog now."

"And a pooper scooper."

Karen wasn't athletic, but she did her best, jogging, even taking a stab at indoor tennis. Irish spent most of the time giving Ricky a lesson. Afterward she introduced them to Doris and Derek. Everyone got along and they went out to dinner. Doris protested, "This is the greatest mistake of my life. What possesses me to even think of letting my husband near any woman who looks like Karen Chambers?" Mutual laughter had hardly subsided when Doris rendered another line. "Karen, I want you to know Derek's simply awful in bed, very boring. You wouldn't like him."

When Karen and Ricky left Sunday evening, Irish felt her full measure of loneliness. Even Sam seemed dejected. "Just you and me, kid." She bent down and hugged him. "We're going to be all right. We're tough guys."

That evening she busied herself catching up on her correspondence, writing to her uncle and aunt in California, then to Heather Whiting. She was attending computer programming school in Boston. Her last letter said her friend Doug was just that, a friend, but she had a classmate at school who was. . . . Irish smiled as she reread the letter. Heather never had finished the sentence, indicating all manner of possibilities. She did say he was deaf. Irish wondered how much speech he had. Did they talk in sign? She asked all that in her letter.

Finally, she replied to a letter from Rose and Edgar Easton, old friends who lived near Pittsfield, Mass. Their son Greg was in college, which Irish found hard to believe. In her letter she decried that she was getting old if Greg was in college. She commented on the other children, asking particularly about Maureen, the oldest daughter now at home. Then she reported some news about her own activity. Before signing, she promised to visit them now that the weather was warmer.

In none of the letters did she mention Geoff Winter. She knew all would wonder, for she'd raved about him in previous letters. Somehow she didn't want to make explanations. She figured they'd get the message anyway.

When she finished her run with Sam late Friday afternoon, Geoff was waiting for her on the porch. It was a warm spring day and she had worked up a generous sweat.

"Seems we met like this before."

She could only stare at him, struggling for

breath. She knew she was winded from her run; still, her need for air seemed excessive.

"It's good to see you, Irish," he said, his blue gaze caressing her.

She walked past him into the house, leaving him to pet Sam, who was wagging his tail ecstatically and jumping on him. She went straight to the refrigerator and poured orange juice, something she always did. Then she did something different. She stood at the sink, her back to the rest of the house, her mind a whirl of emotions. There were too many, all vying for dominance, and she knew only confusion. After draining the glass, she set it on the counter, rather hard, actually, and turned around to face him. He was standing by the door, looking at her, his face expectant. He wore a blue blazer, pink sports shirt, no tie. He had come for the weekend. Certainly not to spend it with her! "Why did you come?"

"I had to. This has gone on long enough, Irish."

She felt herself tremble. From what? Anger, gratitude—he looked so good—fear of him, herself, herself with him? His eyes drew her to him.

"How are you?"

She found her voice. "I'm fine."

"You look well."

She glanced down at her sweat suit, started to speak, then remembered. It had been the same when they first met. She would not reenact it. "There's no point to this, Geoff."

"Yes, there is. I love you and you love me. I can't go on this way. I have an idea you can't either."

"I can and I will. You're just making it worse."

"You're a tough lady, Irish. I thought you'd be back before the first week was out. I should have

169

known you wouldn't. Isn't stubbornness an Irish trait?"

"It isn't stubbornness." She pursed her lips. "It's over, Geoff. I've accepted it. It makes it easier for me. I suggest you leave and do likewise."

He shook his head. "No, it's not over." He bent, rather casually, and gave the ears of a beseeching Sam a rub. From a squatting position he looked up at her and said, "I've been busy while you've been gone."

"So I hear. Karen told me."

"You've seen her?"

"She and Ricky came out last weekend. We had a nice time."

"I'm glad for you. I'm glad you and Karen are good friends." He stood up now. "Aren't you going to ask what I've been doing?"

"I really don't much care." Then she sighed. "Geoff, I don't want to be nasty. I don't want to quarrel. I just want you to leave."

"I've been house hunting. I've narrowed the choices down to a half dozen which—"

"You're kidding!"

"I want you to make your choice. There's still some daylight. We could do a couple today, the rest tomorrow."

She couldn't believe him. "Houses? For us?"

"Of course."

She shook her head. "You're unbelievable! Can't you get it through your thick head that—"

"No, I can't and I won't."

Again she shook her head. "I get it. This is some kind of bribe. You'll show me some houses—real nice places—then I fall into your arms and live happily ever after."

He grinned. "Something like that."

170

She was shaking with anger. He was insufferable, so sure of himself. "And the two children we're to *adopt?*"

"They're on hold—but not too much longer. Actually, that's why I'm here today. If we want them, we have to take them soon."

"I don't *want* them."

"You will when you meet them. I have. They're lovely, really super. The girl has blonde—"

"Stop it! Nothing has changed, has it? I'm still unfit to be a mother." She felt so hurt she was close to tears, and realized she must be shrieking. "I can't live with a man who has no faith in me. I've spent all these years overcoming my handicap, finding confidence. You're destroying it—destroying *me*. I won't have it."

"That's crazy, Irish, and you know it." He started to come to her, then restrained himself. "It's not a case of fitness. It's a matter of facing certain facts, recognizing what's possible and what isn't. You *do* have limitations, whether you want to think so or not. You can't be a music critic or—"

"A mother." She shook her head in despair, her momentary anger suddenly replaced by futility. "We've already had this argument, Geoff. There's no sense in repeating it. Why don't you just leave— leave me, leave us, leave our pleasant memories intact."

He stared at her, and she could see he was trying to control his anger. Toward that end he turned away and went to her easel. He appeared to be looking at it, but she knew he wasn't. When he turned back to her he appeared calmer.

"You were right in the beginning, Irish. All those problems. So much to get used to. I'd simply never realized how much two people depend upon hearing to communicate. The telephone, for example, how important that is. And you were mostly right about me. I was treating you differently. I was too protective, too attentive. I was monitoring everything you said. I was acting like you couldn't get along without me. It must have been smothering for you." He sighed. "But I'd like to think I improved, learned to relax, stopped worrying about you, just enjoyed being with you."

"Yes, you did."

"And the communication problem was awful. I couldn't let you know when my plans changed, and you couldn't let me know where you were. We had a couple of good ones about that. But as bad as that problem was, we solved it. You have to admit the teletype was a good idea."

"Yes, a heavenly instrument."

"We've come so far, Irish. Can't we go a bit further and work out this next problem? We both want children. Can't we find some way to have them, love them, and not quarrel like this?"

She watched him closely, blinking a little to be sure she was seeing him correctly. He was not pleading with her, nor did she want him to. He was too manly for that. What he was being was reasonable. That was certainly a change. "That's a bit different. Up to now you've been making pronouncements on how I can't raise children. You've been *saving* me from myself. Now the subject's open for discussion. To answer your question, yes, we can solve our problem. Forgive me, I can't help calling it *your* problem."

He seemed surprised. "We can? Really?"

"Yes. There's a very easy solution—just have children the way everybody else does."

"Not that again."

"Yes, again—and again. Everybody knows deaf parents can raise hearing children."

"Who's everybody?"

"Doris and Karen, to name two. Both say I ought to educate you. Karen suggested I send you an article or book on the subject. I don't know what Doris has in mind—except maybe have a couple of kids by somebody and call you twenty years later to see how well I did."

"That's silly. Look, I think you'll make a wonderful mother. I don't think, I know. But I just can't see how you can take care of babies, real little ones. You won't—"

"You told me—all the crying. They'll talk funny."

He brightened with an idea. "If seven and nine is too old, maybe we could find them younger, four or five, maybe even three. How's that for a compromise?"

"Lousy." She sighed. "If I could only convince you. Sure, deaf mothers have special problems with their children, but they are all easily solved. I know people who—" She stopped, wide-eyed. Of course. Why hadn't she thought of it before? Abruptly she walked toward the bedroom.

"Where're you going?"

"I'm going to shower and change, then we're going for a drive. I'm about to educate you."

"Now?"

"Yes. Do you want to drive or shall I?"

He shrugged in puzzlement. "I'll drive, but this is crazy."

TEN

She had him drive to Wilton then head north on
Route 7. They drove in silence for a while, Sam
between them in the front seat, then Geoff said,
"May I ask where we're going?"

"Up to the Berkshires, near Pittsfield, Mass."

"Nice drive. What's the point?"

"Maybe none, but it's all I can think of."

"You make it sound ominous, as though it's the
last mile with me. Is it?"

"I don't know. I hope not."

"Does it have to do with me—with us?"

She laughed. "No more questions. Allow me
some mystery. Let's talk about something else.
How's your actor friend, Kevin O'Neill?"

He began to regale her with Hollywood stories.
Seems Kevin O'Neill had a son by a former marriage. There was a nasty custody battle with his ex-
wife, whom O'Neill considered little more than a
tramp. He had the child, but she kept dragging him
through the courts, mindless of the effect on their
son. Geoff's task was to set up and administer a
trust fund O'Neill had set up for the boy.

Listening to him, she felt a sense of peace and
belonging. Geoff Winter really was the most interesting man she knew. They nearly always had something to talk about. Memories flooded over her. He
was such a good man, such a special man. He made
her whole. Without him, she now knew, she was

174

incomplete. *Please God, let this trip work for Geoff and me.*

The hour's drive passed quickly and soon she had him turn off Route 7 into a small town. "It's not far now."

"Irish, I think I have a right to know where we're going and what we're doing."

"We're going to visit friends of mine, Edgar and Rose Easton. He's a tool and die maker, quite a good one. Rose is a bookkeeper."

"And why?"

"You'll see." She had him turn into a lovely street graced with turn-of-the-century homes. Daffodils were in bloom and the sugar maples which lined the street were starting to bud. She peered ahead. "There, on the right, the blue house. I think we can park in front." As he did so, she forgot him momentarily in her excitement at seeing the Eastons.

"It's a gorgeous house, Irish."

"Yes, I just love it." It was three-story, rambling, with a cupola and captain's walk. A commodious porch, reached by stairs, circled the front. "It used to be white, but I sort of like the federal blue with white trim."

"Just the sort of place I want for us."

She glanced at him, blinked. "Shall we go in?"

They were at the bottom of the porch stairs when the front door opened and what seemed a herd of children burst out, screaming, "Irish, Irish!" Then she was smothered in arms and young bodies, surrounded by a cacophony of squeals which only Geoff could hear. He watched, quite amused, and counted—four, no five children. Ages ranged from six or seven to fifteen or so.

Irish, who had squatted to hug the youngest, now stood up, well supported by arms around her hips

175

and waist. She smiled at Geoff, her eyes bright, dancing. "Isn't this a bunch? Let me introduce you. Kids, this is my friend Geoff Winter from New York. Geoff this is—" she touched the head of the boy on her right. "—Denny Easton. How old are you now?"

"Eight."

"Already? And this one is Evelyn. If Denny's eight, you must be ten."

"I was eleven last week."

"And this one over here, George, has to be—let me see—fourteen?"

"Not till August."

"You're in the ninth grade now?"

"Eighth. I go to high school next year."

"Time does fly. I don't know these other ragamuffins." The word was greeted with laughter. "They must be friends."

They were, but identities were lost as a half dozen spoke at once.

"We were playing Monopoly."

"Were you? Who was winning?" The question received no answer for at that moment Irish saw an older girl emerge from the house. She wore an apron and was wiping her hands on a dish towel. Irish gaped at her. "Oh, Maureen!" She went to her and they hugged, then Irish stood back, arms on her shoulders, looking at her, shaking her head in wonder. "You're so beautiful!" And she was, with shining brown hair and lovely sloe eyes now luminous at seeing her visitor. "Seventeen?"

"Yes."

Irish hugged her again. "You must fight off boys with a club."

Maureen laughed. "Only some. Mom and Dad will be home shortly. They'll be so glad to see you."

Irish saw her glance at Geoff. "This is my friend Geoff Winter. Maureen Easton."

Geoff grinned at her. "Irish has a tendency toward understatement. You're a little more than beautiful." Her shy smile was a mixture of delight and innocence.

Everyone trooped into the house. The interior went with the outside, a little antiquey with beautiful oak woodwork, even glass doorknobs. It exuded comfort. Nothing fancy or very new. The place was lived in. While the neighbor kids put on their coats and left, Maureen led Irish and Geoff out to the kitchen. It was large, warm, and commodious, a regular country kitchen. There was even a huge, old-fashioned fireplace although no longer used for cooking. "I'm fixing dinner. You will stay, won't you?"

Irish smiled. "Only if you'll let me help." She saw the vegetables on the counter. "I'm a great potato peeler."

Geoff was given a beer from the refrigerator and instructed to sit at the maple kitchen table with the evening paper. But he didn't get a chance to read, as Denny, Evelyn, and George beseiged him with questions. Was he really from New York City? Where did he live? Did he like living there? What did he do? What's a tax lawyer?

"Are you and Irish gonna get married?" It came from Denny who was playing with Sam.

Geoff grinned. He looked at Irish, then back at Denny. "I don't know. We'll have to see."

Maureen scolded her little brother. "You shouldn't ask such questions, Denny."

"Why not? I wanted to know."

Geoff burst out laughing. "As a matter of fact, so do I."

"There's Mom and Dad."

Car headlights flashing in the approaching darkness confirmed Evelyn's statement, and in a moment Rose and Edgar Easton had entered the kitchen through the back door, surprised and delighted to see Irish. There were hugs and kisses all around.

Rose Easton looked to be in her early fifties, her husband a few years older. He was tallish, slender, and quite bald, with a Caesar's wreath of short-cropped gray hair around the pate. He had no apparent eyebrows, which gave him a perpetual look of surprise. His green eyes were warm and his smile friendly. Rose Easton had dark hair, streaked with gray, dark eyes, and a fleshy face which bore the imprint of early beauty. Her figure was ample. The effect of her was motherliness.

Geoff was momentarily forgotten. Irish had her back to him, deeply immersed in conversation with Rose and Edgar, both of whom were intent on her. Then Irish turned to him, her face radiant. "Geoff, I want you to meet my dear, dear friends, Rose and Edgar Easton."

Smiling, Geoff stood up and strode across the kitchen to shake the outstretched hand of Edgar Easton.

"How do you do?"

Geoff blinked. The man's voice was peculiar. It sounded strained and unnatural. He turned to Rose, bowing slightly. She smiled back warmly, but did not speak. Then he looked at Irish, the fingers of her right hand moving rapidly. When her eyes met his they were serious, full of doubt.

"I—I spelled your name . . . told them you're my friend . . . from New York."

Geoff swallowed. "Your friends are deaf?"

178

"Yes." She turned away, signing to the Eastons with both hands. When they nodded, she said to Geoff, "I asked them if it was all right to tell you about them. Rose and Edgar were born deaf. They have some speech. But they weren't taught as children, and it is difficult to learn at an older age. They feel more comfortable using sign."

Geoff stared at her. "I didn't know you knew sign."

"Oh, yes." She smiled. "But I don't use it a lot. I'm afraid I'm rusty." She smiled at Maureen who was busy signing to her parents. "Look at Maureen. Now, *she's* good."

Another flurry of signs came, leaving Geoff bewildered, but actions revealed that it had to do with staying for dinner, fixing the meal, and Edgar changing his work clothes. Geoff retreated to his former place at the table and watched a highly domestic scene, filled with happy chatter both spoken —between Irish and Maureen—and in sign when Rose was involved. It was a fascinating mixture to Geoff.

In a few minutes Irish came to sit with him. "I think I'm more hindrance than help. Are you surprised?"

He looked at her levelly. "I have to say I am."

"You only know the half of it. Rose and Edgar have eight children. Four have left home." She named them. The oldest son and daughter were married, both parents, the next two in college.

"All can hear?"

"Yes, every one of them—and each one is marvelous." She saw him nod and knew he was getting the message she hoped he would. "What's your impression of Maureen?"

He looked at her. She was at the range, its burn-

179

ers filled with assorted pans and kettles. A large roast, just out of the oven and ready for carving, was the centerpiece. "She's lovely, very nice."

"What else?"

He watched as she called to her little brother to leave Sam and wash his hands for dinner. Denny came in protesting they weren't dirty. Maureen told him to wash them anyway. "And use soap. It won't hurt you."

Geoff turned back to Irish. "What am I supposed to be seeing?"

"Maureen is the oldest child still at home. As such she is the voice of her parents—and a whole lot more. Right, Maureen?"

The girl turned to them. "I'm sort of assistant mother, assistant cook, assistant housekeeper. But I don't mind."

Irish laughed. "Denny give you a hard way to go?"

"Sometimes." She smiled. "I am only his sister, after all. He never lets me forget it. But if he's too bad I turn him over to Mom and Dad." She turned to her mother, who was at the sink, and signed to her. Rose replied, then Maureen said, "Mom says I'm too hard on him, but then she doesn't know everything I do." She laughed. "He can't help it he's the youngest and one hundred percent boy."

"He's that, all right." Irish turned to Geoff. "In families of the deaf, a lot of responsibility falls on the oldest child. They hear for the parents, speak for the parents. They look after the younger children."

Maureen interrupted. "The orders really come from the folks. I sort of execute them." She smiled. "It's hard sometimes—after school before the folks come home. Problems come up and I'm not sure how to handle them. I'm not always right."

Geoff asked, "Do Denny, Evelyn, and George know sign?"

"Oh, yes. They learn it very young." She laughed. "They want direct access to Mom and Dad."

Irish saw him nod his understanding, then she said, "The responsibility for the others is passed from child to child. It's Maureen's turn now." To her she said, "You'll be going to college in the fall?"

"Yes, Boston College, I hope. Then it's George's turn."

Eight of them sat down to dinner in the kitchen, a wholesome "groaning board" of roast beef, mashed potatoes and gravy, several vegetables, homemade bread, and apple pie. It was heavenly for Irish. She had such a sense of family and fun, and she felt renewed, even though she felt pangs of grief for loss of her own family. Geoff sat between Maureen and Evelyn and seemed to have so much fun laughing and talking with them and the other children. She was surprised at first, then remembered he was really a Polish boy from a large family. No wonder he acted so much at home.

The meal seemed to end too quickly. George, Evelyn, and Denny were going to a basketball game at the high school. Maureen would have gone, but elected to stay home because Irish was there. When the kids had their coats on and were headed for the door, Edgar stopped them, motioning vigorously in sign. Irish watched and understood, then explained to Geoff.

"Edgar's asking them what time they're coming home." She observed a moment, then laughed. "It seems they're having a negotiation. Edgar's all for ten-thirty, but George is holding out for midnight. There's a school dance after the game." More signing. "George is appealing to his mother." She smiled. "It's all settled. Evelyn will bring Denny home at ten-thirty. George can stay out an hour longer."

Geoff laughed. "Sounds like my family when I was growing up."

"There's a difference, though. It's all right tonight because Maureen's here—and you."

"Me?"

"Yes." Irish studied him. "Think about it."

Maureen waited a moment then said, "The telephone, Mr. Winter. You and I can answer it. If one of my brothers or sisters is late, changes plans, or is in any kind of trouble, he can phone."

Geoff smiled. "How can you do that—speak to me and sign to your parents at the same time?"

"Practice."

Rose interrupted with a cutting motion of her hand, then began to speak in sign. Irish translated for Geoff. "The hardest thing for her is to have the children out of sight. She worries constantly." Rose shook her head. "She says she even worries about the older ones that are away from home. If anything happens to them she won't know, won't be able to help them."

Edgar interrupted his wife and Irish translated that, too. "He says she worries too much."

Then Irish spoke for herself. "The point is, Geoff, deaf parents really have to know where their children are, if it's school, a friend's house, wherever. And they'd better come home when they're supposed to."

Rose, who was both reading lips and watching

182

Maureen's sign, laughed and made a spanking motion.

"It really is strict discipline." Irish asked Maureen if that wasn't so.

"Oh, yes. But we all realize there's a good reason for it. Mom and Dad are never punitive or excessive. They just let us know what's expected of us. They trust us to live up to it."

Geoff eyed her a moment. "Is that hard for you?"

"Sometimes. I'd like to go off with my friends, but know I have to be home." She smiled. "It's all right. Can't be helped. I think it was probably worse for Jim and Eileen, the oldest."

"Why so?"

Maureen laughed. "Mom and Dad are a lot more relaxed than they used to be."

While Maureen cleared the table, the four of them began a new, if similar, conversation. Irish started it, signing to Rose, "Will you tell Geoff what it was like when Jim was born? You couldn't hear him. How did you manage?" She paused, reading Rose's reply. "Yes, of course I know, but I'd like for Geoff to know it."

"My education?"

She smiled at him. "Never too late to learn."

He looked at her earnestly. "I don't want it to be too late."

Irish blinked. Oh, how she wanted that to be so! She turned back to Rose, watching her reply, then spoke aloud for Geoff's benefit. "Rose says she was terrible. She knew nothing about babies and was scared to death." Irish smiled, then signed a question to Rose. "She was only eighteen when her first child was born. I hadn't known that." Irish paused to watch Rose's artistic hand motions. "She and Edgar didn't have much money—only love. Since she couldn't hear Jim cry, she tried to keep him in sight at all times. The playpen or stroller was moved from room to room. She took him with her when she went to the basement or outside to hang up clothes—the store, wherever she went. When he took his nap, she'd frequently sit beside him, knitting or ironing or something. Otherwise she went into the room every five minutes or so to see if he was crying or awake."

"What about night?"

Irish signed Geoff's question to Rose, then uttered her reply. "She and Edgar slept with the baby between them so they could feel him crying for a bottle or a diaper change."

Edgar interrupted and Irish translated that. "Edgar says it is much easier today. There are devices which automatically turn a light on, awakening the parents, when the baby cries or begins to thrash around." Irish looked at Rose. "She says that such devices probably existed when Jim was a baby, but they couldn't afford it. They slept with the baby for over two years, then he was old enough to wake them himself if he needed or wanted anything. He could sleep in his own bed then."

"That young?"

"Oh, yes, Geoff. Children of the deaf learn very young that their parents can't hear and compensate for it."

Geoff looked at Maureen who was pouring fresh coffee. "Is that true?"

"Yes. I can't remember when I didn't know. I never thought about it." She smiled. "I guess I thought all parents were that way."

"Were you surprised to discover—"

"That other parents can hear? Not really. Don't

184

all kids accept and love their parents however they are?"

Irish watched Geoff's eyes and loved what she saw, then she turned to Rose, signed a question, and told Geoff the reply. "I asked Rose how Jim learned to speak. She says it mostly just happened. He heard other kids, neighbors, relatives who dropped by. The summer before he was three he spent a great deal of time with Rose's sister Catherine and her family. Rose said she always was told he spoke very well, even when he was young." Irish smiled. "Her dearest wish is that she might hear the voices of her children. Perhaps in heaven, she says." Irish's eyes misted over and she felt a choking sensation in her own throat.

She felt Maureen's comforting hand on her shoulder and looked up to see her speaking to Geoff. "It's not possible to exaggerate the importance of the firstborn to deaf parents, Mr. Winter."

"Geoff, please. I'm not old enough to have sweet young things call me mister."

"Okay, Geoff it is." She smiled. "By the time my brother Jim was two, maybe even before that, he was the ears and voice of Mom and Dad. Think of what that meant. He could answer the door, talk to strangers. They could have a telephone. He made everything so much easier for them." As Maureen spoke she was signing to her parents. Now she watched her father's hands a moment, then said, "Dad says no subsequent children were as difficult as the first. When Eileen was born she slept in the room with Jim. He could awaken them in the night if she cried. Because he spoke, Eileen learned naturally. We all learned from our brothers and sisters, not from Mom and Dad."

Geoff seemed agitated then, unable to sit; he got

up from the table and walked across the kitchen, as though deep in thought. When he turned he spoke to Irish. "I'm beginning to understand why you were so upset with me."

"You were very silly."

He nodded. "Ignorant. I just didn't know."

"Few people do. I don't know if there are statistics or not, but as a group, children of the deaf are considered more successful than the general population. Lots of very good people in business, the professions, arts, have been children of the deaf. I think there were even one or two presidents. Know why?"

"Let me think." He made another pace across the kitchen, turned, looked at Rose and Edgar and Maureen, then at Irish. "I suppose it's what you said —and did tonight. Knowing where the kids are, what they're doing, having them come home at a specified time. They just have to be less self-centered and—" he hesitated for the right word "—responsible. Is that what you're talking about?"

"Only part of it, Geoff. Remember, deaf parents can't hear the child. Rose kept her children in sight as much as she could. This means children of the deaf receive a tremendous dose of parental attention. Neglected is the last thing they ever are."

Geoff nodded his head vigorously in understanding. "Combine the two, lots of attention and a sense of responsibility for others, and you have a remarkable individual."

Maureen was smiling. "My brother Jim is on the faculty of MIT. He teaches electrical engineering. Eileen is a resident in pediatrics at Massachusetts General Hospital. Her husband is also a doctor. Ben is a senior at UMass and is on the dean's list."

She smiled. "Too early to tell much about Doug. I think he's the black sheep."

Irish laughed. "Hardly. He's my favorite." She looked at Geoff. "I think there's something else that benefits the children of the deaf." Out of the corner of her eye she saw Edgar motioning and turned to him, nodding at the message his hands wrote. "Edgar says his children all have an awareness of human limitations and what must be done to surmount them. They have a greater tolerance of people who are different and—"

Geoff interrupted. "A sense of what it takes to get along, with others, work with them." His eyes moved from Irish to Maureen and back. "Know what impresses me the most?"

Irish smiled. "I'd like to know."

He looked at Maureen, his gaze very direct, open. "You. You're extraordinarily mature for seventeen. All that cooking, looking after the children I guess." He smiled. "The man who gets you has won a prize."

She said he was embarrassing her, but her smile belied that.

They were alone in the living room. All of the Eastons had gone to bed, doubtless to give them a few minutes of privacy. Edgar had built a fire, which was now dying to embers. Sam lay before it, sopping up the heat.

Irish sat on the couch. "I've never seen a dog like a fire as much as Sam."

"He's a Lab, isn't he? It's cold up there." He was standing before the fire, too, a nightcap in his hand.

"You sure you don't mind spending the night? I never thought to bring clothes or anything."

187

"It's all right. I want to explore some of this countryside in the morning."

"Yes, it is beautiful." She hesitated. "It'll be easier to drive back in daylight."

"Yes."

All this was small talk and both knew it. Irish felt a strange heat, and it wasn't from the fire. It was as though her body was trying to send a message to a still reluctant mind. She looked up at Geoff, meeting his gaze, so penetrating, so deep. She felt full of anticipation.

"I've been a damn fool, Irish. Can you forgive me?"

"There's nothing to forgive."

"Oh, yes, there is. These are wonderful people, a wonderful family. Being around them I realize just how far I've strayed from home. I wanted to escape my roots. I wanted to be better. I wanted success and sophistication."

"That you have."

"But at too high a price—so far at least. Living in Manhattan, associating with the people I do—'the beautiful people,' you forget just how many marvelous people there are who don't live that way. In a word, I'm a bit humbler right now. I'd like to take you back home to meet my family."

She swallowed, not an entirely easy act at this emotional moment. "I've wanted to do that."

"There's another thing. I've realized tonight I really have been prejudiced about you." He saw her shaking her head. "Yes, it's true, Irish. Maybe I wasn't consciously aware of it, but I really did feel superior to you because of your deafness. At least I acted superior. You couldn't get along without me." He shook his head, as though disbelieving his own actions and attitudes. "Hell, Irish, you get along better than I do. Can you forgive me?"

She felt her eyes burn, then the coolness of tears. "It's not a case of forgiving, Geoff, but of understanding." He nodded, several times, then sat beside her on the couch, very close, taking both her hands in one of his where they rested in her lap. She knew he was speaking, and turned a little so she could see his lips.

"I wish I could explain how I feel." He sighed. "I'm not sure I understand myself." He pressed his lips into a hard line. "Cleansed, I guess—cleansed of prejudice and arrogance and ignorance." His gaze rose to hers. "I love you, Irish O'Brien."

She tried to blink the tears away and finally freed a hand to wipe at her eyes, quickly returning it to the smooth, magnetic touch of his hand. "You're too hard on yourself." She smiled. "I won't have anyone saying nasty things about the man I love."

"Do you really love me, Irish?"

"Remember I told you when I said the words it would be forever and ever? I meant that. I've never stopped loving you."

He grinned. "Maybe it's just a bit easier now?"

"Oh my, yes. Maybe that's not good. I'm not sure I'll be able to stand someone so likeable. I won't have anything to fight with you about."

"We'll think of something."

His lips beckoned her. As she leaned forward toward that beautiful mouth, so familiar now, she felt the sweetness of renewal as she was joined to him. His arms came around her and she felt a sense of relief, as though her whole body were sighing.

In a few moments she moved her head back to see what he was saying. "Do you really have to sleep with Maureen?"

She smiled, " 'Fraid so—and you with Denny. A good night's sleep will do you good."

"No, it won't. Okay, so it can't be helped. But why don't we try to leave about noon tomorrow? We can get back in time to look at a couple of those houses, then we can—"

"You do have the best ideas."